"**What you're asking us to do is the complete opposite of London Connection's mission statement. I'll have to discuss this with my colleagues before accepting.**"

"I don't want your colleagues," Luca said. "The fewer people who know what I'm asking, the better. I want *you*."

His words and the intensity of his blue eyes were charging into her like a shock of electricity, leaving Amy trying to catch her breath without revealing he'd knocked it out of her.

"I don't understand." It was common knowledge that the new king of Vallia was nothing like the previous one. Luca's father had been... Well, he'd been dubbed "the Kinky King" by the tabloids, so that said it all.

Amy's distant assumption when she had recognized Luca was that she would be tasked with finessing some remnant of Luca's father's libidinous reputation. Even so... "To the best of my knowledge, your image is spotless. Why would you *want* a scandal?"

Signed, Sealed...Seduced

Billion-dollar deals and breathtaking passion!

At boarding school, Clare, Bea and Amy formed an unbreakable bond. Years later, they're making waves as the owners of their own successful PR company. But having billionaires for clients means the most unexpected tasks...and *temptation*...can be thrown in their paths at a moment's notice!

Amy is sent to the Mediterranean kingdom of Vallia by the unusual request to ruin King Luca's image. What she doesn't expect is to be the center of the scandal!

Read more in
Ways to Ruin a Royal Reputation by Dani Collins

Shy Bea is left alone to handle their most important client, Ares! First job: accompany him to a Venetian ball...

Find out more in
Cinderella's Night in Venice by Clare Connelly

After escaping from criminals, Clare stows away on tycoon Dev's yacht. When he finds her, they have a convenient deal to strike!

Read on in
The Playboy's "I Do" Deal by Tara Pammi

Dani Collins

WAYS TO RUIN A ROYAL REPUTATION

Special thanks and acknowledgment are given to Dani Collins
for her contribution to the Signed, Sealed...Seduced miniseries

HARLEQUIN®
PRESENTS®

Recycling programs
for this product may
not exist in your area.

ISBN-13: 978-1-335-40401-5

Ways to Ruin a Royal Reputation

Copyright © 2021 by Harlequin Books S.A.

For questions and comments about the quality of this book,
please contact us at CustomerService@Harlequin.com.

Harlequin Enterprises ULC
22 Adelaide St. West, 40th Floor
Toronto, Ontario M5H 4E3, Canada
www.Harlequin.com

Printed in U.S.A.

Canadian **Dani Collins** knew in high school that she wanted to write romance for a living. Twenty-five years later, after marrying her high school sweetheart, having two kids with him, working at several generic office jobs and submitting countless manuscripts, she got The Call. Her first Harlequin novel won the Reviewers' Choice Award for Best First in Series from *RT Book Reviews*. She now works in her own office, writing romance.

Books by Dani Collins

Harlequin Presents

Cinderella's Royal Seduction
A Hidden Heir to Redeem Him
Confessions of an Italian Marriage
Innocent in the Sheikh's Palace
What the Greek's Wife Needs

Once Upon a Temptation

Beauty and Her One-Night Baby

One Night With Consequences

Innocent's Nine-Month Scandal
Bound by Their Nine-Month Scandal

Secret Heirs of Billionaires

The Maid's Spanish Secret

Visit the Author Profile page
at Harlequin.com for more titles.

To my fellow authors in this trilogy, Clare Connelly and Tara Pammi.

Writing is a strange beast and can be lonely at times, but when a fun project like this one comes along, it reminds me I have watercooler colleagues who know exactly how my workday is going.

I can't wait until we can get together to celebrate these books in person!

CHAPTER ONE

"RUIN ME."

Amy Miller blinked, certain she'd misheard Luca Albizzi, the king of Vallia.

She'd been reeling since she'd walked into this VIP suite in London's toniest hotel and discovered who her potential client would be.

Her arrival here had been conducted under a cloak of mystery. A call had had her assistant frowning with perplexity as she relayed the request that Amy turn up for an immediate consultation, now or never.

Given the address, Amy had been confident it was worth pandering to the vague yet imperious invitation. It wasn't unheard-of for managers of celebrities to conceal a client's identity while they brought Amy and her team into a crisis situation.

Amy had snatched up her bag and hurried across the city, expecting to meet an outed MP's son or an heiress being blackmailed with revenge porn.

The hotel manager had brought her to the Royal Suite, a title Amy had not taken seriously despite the pair of men guarding the door, both wearing dark suits and inscrutable expressions. One had searched through her satchel while the other inspected the jacket she had nervously removed in the lift.

When they opened the door for her, Amy had warily entered an empty lounge.

As she set her bag and jacket on a bar stool, the sound of the main door closing had brought a pensive man from one of the bedrooms.

He wore a bone-colored business shirt over dark gray trousers, no tie, and had such an air of authority, he nearly knocked her over with it. He was thirtyish, swarthy, his hair light brown, his blue eyes piercing enough to score lines into her.

Before she had fully recognized him, a hot, bright pull twisted within her. A sensual vine that wound through her limbs slithered to encase her, and yanked.

It was inexplicable and disconcerting—even more so when her brain caught up to realize exactly who was provoking this reaction.

The headlines had been screaming for weeks that the Golden Prince, recently crowned the king of Vallia, would be coming to London on a state visit. King Luca had always been notorious for the fact he was powerful, privileged and sinfully good-looking. Everything else about him was above reproach. According to reports, he'd dined at Buckingham Palace last night where the only misstep had been a smoky look of admiration from a married duchess that he had ignored.

"Call me Luca," he said by way of introduction, and invited her to sit.

Gratefully, Amy had sunk onto the sofa, suffering the worst case of starstruck bedazzlement she'd ever experienced. She spoke to wealthy and elite people all the time and never lost her tongue. Or her hearing. Or her senses. She refused to let this man be anything different, but he was. He just was.

She saw his mouth move again. The words he'd just spoken were floating in her consciousness, but his gorgeously deep voice with that Italian accent evoked hot humid nights in narrow cobblestone alleys while romantic strains of a violin drifted from open windows. She could practically smell the fragrance of exotic blossoms weighting the air. He would draw her into a shadowed alcove and that full-lipped, hot mouth would smother—

"Will you?" he prodded.

Amy yanked herself back from the kind of fantasy that could, indeed, ruin him. *And* her. He was a potential client, for heaven's sake!

A cold tightness arrived behind her breastbone as she made the connection that she was, once again, lusting for someone off-limits. Oh, God. She wouldn't say the king of Vallia reminded her of *him*. That would be a hideous insult. Few men were as reprehensible as *him*, but a clammy blanket of apprehension settled on her as she realized she was suffering a particularly strong case of the butterflies for someone who potentially had power over her.

She forcibly cocooned those butterflies and reminded herself she was not without power of her own. She could turn down this man or this job. In fact, based on this off-the-rails attraction she was suffering, she should do both.

She would, once she politely heard him out. At the very least, she could recommend one of her colleagues.

Why did *that* thought make this weird ache in her diaphragm pang even harder?

She shook it off.

"I'm sorry," she said, managing to dredge the words from her dry throat. "Did you say someone is trying to ruin you? London Connection can definitely help you defuse that." There. She almost sounded like the savvy, confident, cofounder of a public relations firm that her business card said she was.

"I said I want *you* to ruin me."

You. Her heart swerved. *Did he know?* Her ears grew so hot, she feared they'd set her hair on fire. He couldn't know what had happened, she assured herself even as snakes of guilt and shame writhed in her stomach. Her parents and the school's headmistress had scrubbed out that little mess with all the alacrity of a government cleanup team in a blockbuster movie. That's how Amy had learned mistakes could be mitigated so well they disappeared from the collective consciousness, even if the stain remained on your conscience forever.

Nevertheless, her hands clenched in her lap as though she had to physically hang on to all she'd managed to gain after losing everything except the two best friends who remained her staunchest supporters to this day.

"Our firm is in the business of *building* reputations." Muscle memory came to her rescue, allowing her voice to steady and strengthen. She said this sort of thing a million times a week. "Using various tools like media channels and online networking, we protect and enhance our clients' profiles. When a brand or image has been impacted, we take control of the narrative. Build a story." Blah, blah, blah.

She smiled while she spoke, hands now stacked palm up in her lap, ankles crossed. Her blood still sizzled because, seriously, he was positively magnetic even when he scowled with impatience. This was what a chiseled jaw looked like—as though a block of marble named "naked gold" or "autumn tan" had been chipped and worked and shaped to become this physical manifestation of strength and tenacity. Command.

"I know what you do. That's why I called you." Luca rose abruptly from the armchair he'd taken when she'd sat.

He paced across the spacious lounge. His restless movement ruffled the sheer drapes that were partially drawn over the wall of windows overlooking the Thames.

She'd barely taken in the decor of grays and silver-blue, the fine art pieces and the arrangements of fresh flowers. It all became a monochrome backdrop to a man who radiated a dynamic aura. He moved like an athlete with his smooth, deliberate motions. His beautifully tailored clothes only emphasized how well made he was.

He paused where the spring sun was streaming through the break in the curtains and shoved his hands into his pockets. The action strained his trousers across his firm behind.

Amy was not an ogler. Men of all shapes, sizes and levels of wealth paraded through her world every day. They were employees and clients and couriers. Nothing more. She hadn't completely sworn off emotional entanglements, but she was exceptionally careful. Occasionally she dated, but even the very nice men who paid for dinner and asked politely before trying to kiss her had failed to move her.

Truthfully, she didn't allow anyone to move her. She preferred to keep her focus on her career. She'd been taught by an actual, bona-fide teacher that following her heart, or her libido, or that needy thing inside her that yearned for someone to make her feel special, would only leave her open to being used and thrown away like last week's rubbish.

But here she was acting like a sixth-former biting her fist because a particularly nice backside was in her line of sight. Luca wasn't even coming on to her. He was just oozing sex appeal from his swarthy pores in a passive and oblivious way.

That was ninja-level seduction and it had to stop.

"I'm asking you to reverse the build," Luca said. "Give me a scandal instead of making one go away."

She dragged her attention up to find him looking over his shoulder at her.

He cocked his brow to let her know he had totally and completely caught her drooling over his butt.

She briefly considered claiming he had sat in chewing gum and gave her hair a flick, aware she was as red as an Amsterdam sex district light. She cleared her throat and suggested gamely, "You're in the wrong part of London for cheap disgrace. Possibly hire a woman with a different profession?"

He didn't crack a smile.

She bit the inside of her lip.

"A *controlled* scandal." He turned to face her, hands still in his pockets. He braced his feet apart like a sailor on a yacht, and his all-seeing gaze flickered across her blushing features. "I've done my research. I came to *you* because you're ideal for the job."

Whatever color had risen to her cheeks must have drained out of her because she went absolutely ice cold.

"Why do you say that?" she asked tautly.

His brows tugged in faint puzzlement. "The way you countered the defamation of that woman who was suing the sports league. It was a difficult situation, given how they'd rallied their fans to attack her."

Amy released a subtle breath. He wasn't talking about *her* past.

"It was very challenging," she agreed with a muted nod.

She and her colleagues-slash-best friends, Bea and Clare, had taken on the case for a single pound sterling. They'd all been horrified by the injustice of a woman being vilified because she'd called out some players who had accosted her in a club.

"I'm compelled to point out though—" she lifted a blithe expression to hide the riot going on inside her "—if you wish to be ruined, the firm we were up against in that case specializes in pillorying people."

"Yet they failed with your client because of *your* efforts. How could I even trust them?" He swept a dismissive hand through the air. "They happily billed an obscene amount of money to injure a woman who'd already been harmed. Meanwhile, despite winning, your company lost money with her. Didn't you?"

His piercing look felt like a barbed hook that dug deep into her middle.

Amy licked her lips and crossed her legs. It was another muscle memory move, one she trotted out with men in an almost reflexive way when she felt put on the spot and needed a brief moment of deflection.

It was a power move and it would have worked, buying her precious seconds to choose her words, if she hadn't watched his gaze take note of the way the unbuttoned bottom of her skirt fell open to reveal her shin. His gaze slid down to her ankle and leisurely climbed its way back up, hovering briefly on the open collar of her maxi shirtdress, then arrived at her mouth with the sting of a bee.

As his gaze hit hers, his mouth pulled slightly to one side in a silent, *Thank you for that, but let's stay on task.*

It was completely unnerving and made her stomach wobble. She swallowed, mentally screaming at herself to get her head in the game.

"I would never discuss another client's financial situation." She would, however, send a note to Bea advising her they had some confidentiality holes to plug. "Can you tell me how you came by that impression, though?"

"Your client was quoted in an interview saying that winning in the court of public opinion doesn't pay the way a win in a real court would have done, but thanks to *Amy* at London Connection, she remains hopeful she'll be awarded a settlement that will allow her to pay you what you deserve."

Every nerve ending in Amy's body sparked as he approached. He still seemed edgy beneath his air of restraint. He dropped a slip of paper onto the coffee table in front of her.

"I want to cover her costs as well as my own. Will that amount do?"

The number on the slip nearly had her doing a spit take with the air in her lungs. Whether it was in pounds sterling, euros, or Russian rubles didn't matter. A sum with that many zeroes would have Bea and Clare sending her for a cranial MRI if she turned it down.

"It's...very generous. But what you're asking us to do is the complete opposite of London Connection's mission statement. I'll have to discuss this with my colleagues before accepting." Why did Clare have to be overseas right now? Starting London Connection had been her idea. She'd brought Amy on board to get it off the ground, and they usually made big decisions together. Their latest had been to pry Bea from slow suffocation at a law firm to work for them. Bea might have specific legal concerns about a campaign of this nature.

"I don't want your colleagues," Luca said. "The fewer people who know what I'm asking, the better. I want *you*."

His words and the intensity of his blue eyes were charging into her like a shock of electricity, leaving her trying to catch her breath without revealing he'd knocked it out of her.

"I don't understand." It was common knowledge that the new king of Vallia was nothing like the previous one. Luca's father had been... Well, he'd been dubbed "the Kinky King" by the tabloids, so that said it all.

Amy's distant assumption when she had recognized Luca was that she would be tasked with finessing some remnant of Luca's father's libidinous reputation. Or perhaps shore up the cracks in the new king's image since there were rumors he was struggling under the weight of his new position.

Even so... "To the best of my knowledge, your image is spotless. Why would you *want* a scandal?"

"Have I hired you?" Luca demanded, pointing at the slip of paper. "Am I fully protected under client confidentiality agreements?"

She opened her mouth, struggling to articulate a response as her mind leaped to her five-year plan. If she accepted this assignment, she could reject the trust fund that was supposed to come to her when she turned thirty in eighteen months. Childish, perhaps, but her parents had very ruthlessly withheld it twice in the past. Having learned so harshly that she must rely only on herself, Amy would love to tell them she had no use for the remnants of the family fortune they constantly held out like a carrot on a stick.

Bea and Clare would love a similar guarantee of security. They all wanted London Connection to thrive so they could help people. They most definitely didn't want to tear people down the way some of their competitors did. Amy had no doubt Bea and Clare would have the same reservations she did with Luca's request, but something told her this wasn't a playboy's silly whim. He looked far too grim and resolute.

Coiled through all of this contemplation was an infernal curiosity. Luca intrigued her. If he became a client… Well, if he became a client, he was absolutely forbidden! There was a strange comfort in that. Rules were rules, and Amy would hide behind them if she had to.

"I'll have to tell my partners something," she warned, her gaze landing again on the exorbitant sum he was offering.

"Say you're raising the profile of my charity foundation. It's a legitimate organization that funds mental health programs. We have a gala in a week. I've already used it as an excuse when I asked my staff to arrange this meeting."

"Goodness, if you're that adept at lying, why do you need me?"

Still no glint of amusement.

"It's not a lie. The woman who has been running it since my mother's time fell and broke her hip. The entire organization needs new blood and a boost into this century. You'll meet with the team, double-check the final arrangements and suggest new fundraising programs. The full scope of work I'm asking of you will remain confidential, between the two of us."

His offer was an obscene amount for a few press releases, but Amy could come up with a better explanation for her friends later. Right now, the decision was hers alone as to whether to take the job, and there was no way she could turn down this kind of money.

She licked her dry lips and nodded.

"Very well. If you wish to hire me to promote your charity and fabricate a scandal, I would be happy to be of assistance." She stood to offer her hand for a shake.

His warm, strong hand closed over hers in a firm clasp and gave it a strong pump. The satisfaction that flared in his expression made all sorts of things in her shiver. He was so gorgeous and perfect and un-scathed. Regal.

"Now tell me why on *earth* you would ask me to ruin you," she asked, trying to keep her voice even.

"It's the only way I can give the crown to my sister."

CHAPTER TWO

LUCA RELEASED HER hand with a disturbing sense of reluctance. He quickly dismissed the sexual awareness dancing in his periphery. Amy Miller had a scent of biscotti about her, almonds and anise. It was going to be incredibly distracting to sit with her on the plane, but she was now an employee and he finally had a foot on a path that would allow his sister to take the throne. His entire body twitched to finish the task.

"Eccellente," he said in his country's Italian dialect. "Let's go."

"Go?" Amy fell back a half step and blinked her sea green eyes. "Where?"

"I'm needed in Vallia. We'll continue this conversation on our way."

He glimpsed a flash of panic in her expression, but she quickly smoothed it to show only professional calm.

"I have to take your details first. Prepare and sign the contract. Research—"

Impatience prickled his nape. "I want a secure location before we discuss this further."

"My office is secure. We don't have to go to Vallia." She made it sound like his home was on another planet.

"It's only three hours. My jet is waiting."

Amy's pretty, glossed mouth opened, but nothing came out.

Luca had had his doubts when she had first come onto his radar. He didn't trust anyone who seemed to enjoy being the life of the party, and her job involved nonstop networking with spoiled, infamous attention-seekers. Her online presence was filled with celebrity selfies, club events and influencer-styled posts. It all skated too close for comfort to the superficial amusements his father had pursued with such fervor.

Along with awards and praise from her colleagues, however, she came highly recommended when he'd made a few discreet inquiries. In person, she seemed levelheaded and knowledgeable—if aware of her ability to dazzle with a flick of her more-blond-than-strawberry locks and not the least bit afraid to use such tactics. She was mesmerizing with her peaches and cream skin. Her nose was cutely uptilted to add playfulness to her otherwise aristocratic features, and there was something intangible, a certain sparkle, that surrounded her.

But the very fact she entranced him kept him on his guard. He was long practiced at appreciating the fact a woman was attractive without succumbing to whatever lust she might provoke in him. He was *not* and never would be his father.

Even if he had to convince certain people he was *enough* like him to be undeserving of his crown.

"But—" She waved an exasperated hand. "I have other clients. I can't just drop them all for you."

"Isn't that what I just paid you to do? If you needed more, you should have said."

"You really don't know what my work is, do you?" She frowned with consternation before adding in a disgruntled voice, "I'll have to shift things around. I wish you'd made it clear when you called that you expected me to travel. I would have brought a quick-run bag." She moved to the leather satchel she'd left on a stool at the bar.

"Are you a PR rep or a secret agent?" Luca asked dryly.

"Feels like one and the same most of the time. At least my passport is always in here."

He eyed her slightly-above-average height and perfectly proportioned curves. Amy wore nothing so pedestrian as a skirt suit. No, her rainbow-striped dress was styled like an ankle-length shirt in light-weight silk. She'd rolled back her sleeves to reveal her bangled wrists and left a few buttons open at her throat and below her knees. It was a bohemian yet stylish look that was finished with a black corset-looking device that made him want to take his time unbuckling those five silver tongue and eye closures in the middle of her back. Her black shoes had silver stiletto heels that glinted wickedly, and the shift of filmy silk against her heart-shaped ass was positively erotic.

Not her, Luca reminded himself as a bolt of want streaked from the pit of his gut to the root of his sex. He was woke enough to know that objectifying women was wrong, that women who worked for him were always off-limits, and that grabbing anyone's backside without express permission was unacceptable— even if she'd gawked at his own like she'd wanted to help herself to a handful.

When he'd caught Amy checking him out a few minutes ago, he'd considered scrapping this whole idea in favor of suggesting he refile his flight plan so they could tour the king-size bed in the other room.

Luca didn't place nascent physical attraction over real world obligations, though. Whether it looked like it or not, allowing his sister to take his place was the greatest service he could do for his country. He wouldn't be swayed from it.

If that left room in his future to make a few less than wise decisions with a woman who attracted him, that was icing. For now, he had to keep his mind out of the gutter.

Or rather, only go there in a very shallow and deliberate manner.

Look at the bar Papa set, his twin had sniffed a few weeks ago when he'd been relaying his frustration with the Privy Council's refusal to allow him to abdicate. *You have a long way to sink before they would even think of ousting you in favor of me.*

Luca didn't want to put the country into constitutional crisis or start firing dedicated public servants. He only wanted to make things right, but there were too many people invested in the status quo. He'd tried cultivating a certain incompetence as he'd adopted the duties of king, pushing more and more responsibilities onto Sofia to show she was the more deserving ruler, but the council dismissed his missteps as "adapting to the stress of his new role." They hovered more closely than ever and were driving him mad.

Sofia's casual remark had been effortlessly on the nose, providing Luca with the solution he'd been searching for. He needed to sink to that unforgivable depth in one shot, touch bottom very briefly, then shoot back to the surface before too much damage was done.

Amy Miller was uniquely positioned to help him make that happen, having bailed countless celebrities out of scandals of their own making.

She was helping herself to items from the hospitality basket, dropping an apple and a protein snack into her bag before adding a water bottle and a bar of chocolate.

"I'll deduct this from your bill," she said absently as she examined a lip balm before uncapping it and sweeping it across her naked mouth. She rolled her lips and dropped the tube into her bag. "I'll buy a change of clothes from the boutique in the lobby on our way out."

"We don't have time for a shopping spree. I'll make arrangements for things to be waiting for you when we arrive."

"I'm hideously efficient," she insisted. "Shall I meet you at the front doors in fifteen minutes?" She plucked the black motorcycle jacket off the back of the stool and shrugged it over her dress.

Something in that combination of tough leather over delicate silk, studded black over bright colors, fine blond hair flicked free of the heavy collar and the haughty expression on her face made him want to catch her jacket's lapels in his fists and drag her close for the hottest, deepest kiss of their lives. His heart rate picked up and his chest heated.

Their eyes met, and they were close enough that he saw her pupils explode in reaction to whatever she was reading in his face.

Look at the bar Papa set.

"Car park. Ten minutes." He pushed a gruff coolness into his tone that made it clear he was not invested in her on any level. "Or the whole thing is off."

She flinched slightly, then gave him what he suspected was a stock keep-the-client-happy smile, saying a very unconcerned, "I'll risk it."

It was cheeky enough to grate, mostly because it lit an urgency in him, one that warned him against letting her get away. He started to tell her that when he said something, he meant it, but she was already gone.

* * *

Amy fled the suite. She had reached the limit of her ability to pretend she was cool with all of this and desperately needed to bring her pulse under control, especially after what had just happened.

What *had* just happened?

She had found an excuse to escape his overwhelming presence, dragged on her jacket, glanced at Luca, and a crackling surge of energy between them had nearly sucked her toward him like a tractor beam pulling her into an imploding sun. For one second, she'd thought he was going to leap on her and swallow her whole.

Much to her chagrin, she was a teensy bit disappointed he hadn't. In fact, she was stinging with rejection at the way he'd so quickly frozen her out, as if he hadn't handpicked her to make his worst nightmare come true.

As if she'd been obvious in her attraction toward him and he'd needed to rebuff her.

As if she had consciously been issuing an invitation—which she hadn't!

She was reacting on a purely physical level and was mortified that it was so potent. So *obvious*. She didn't understand why it was happening. Even before all her PR management courses, she'd had a knack for being dropped into a situation that demanded swift, decisive action and turning it around. Now it was her day job to create space for clients to freak out and sob and come to terms with whatever drama might have befallen them. She was adept at processing her own reactions on the fly, but today she was shaking and wishing for a paper bag to breathe into.

Luca was the diametric opposite of everything she'd ever encountered. He wasn't a boy from the council flats who'd stumbled into stardom and didn't know how to handle it. He'd been raised to be king. He was a man of impeccable reputation who wanted her to engineer his fall from grace. Instead of his looks and wealth and privilege getting him into trouble, he needed her to make that happen for him. *I want* you, he'd said.

He'd made it sound as if he saw her as exceptional at what she did, but there was that niggling fear deep in her belly that she'd been chosen for other, bleaker reasons.

Even as she was texting Clare and Bea from the lift, informing them she was leaving town with an important new client who'd offered a "substantial budget," she was stamping her feet to release the emotions that were accosting her.

There was no tricking herself into believing Luca Albizzi was a client like any other. He wasn't. Not just because he was a king. Or because he radiated more sex appeal than a whole calendar of shirtless firefighters. He was…magnificent.

He was causing her to react like a— She pinched the bridge of her nose, hating to admit it to herself, but it was true. She was behaving like damned *schoolgirl*.

That would not do. She was older and wiser than she'd been back then. Infatuation Avenue was firmly closed off. Men were no longer allowed to use her very natural need for affection and companionship as a route to taking advantage of her. Besides, he was a client. Their involvement had to remain strictly professional. It *would*, she vowed.

As the lift doors opened, Clare texted back that she would run things remotely. Bea promised to email their boilerplate for the contract. Neither protested her disappearing, darn them for always being so supportive.

Amy hurried to the boutique. Thankfully, she was blessed with a body that loved off-the-rack clothing. It took longer for the woman to ring up her items than it did for Amy to yank them from the rod. She didn't need to buy a toothbrush. She always kept the grooming basics in her shoulder bag since she often had to freshen up between meetings.

She was catching her breath after racing down the stairs to the car park when the lift bell rang. Luca's bodyguards stepped out. One checked as he saw her hovering, nodding slightly when he recognized her. An SUV slid to a halt, and Luca glanced at her as he appeared and walked across to the door that was opened for him.

"I didn't believe you could find what you wanted in less than an hour." His gaze dropped to the bag she swung as she hurried toward him. "Your ability to follow through on a promise is reassuring."

"Reassurance is the cornerstone of our work. I'm not being facetious. I mean that." She let his bodyguard take her purchases and climbed into the vehicle beside Luca, firmly ignoring the cloud of the king's personal fragrance, which may or may not have been a combination of aftershave, espresso and undiluted testosterone.

Whatever it was, it made her ovaries ache.

As the door shut and the SUV moved up the ramp into the daylight, Amy withdrew her tablet from her satchel, determined to do her job, nothing more, nothing less.

"I was going to look up some background information unless you'd rather brief me yourself?"

He pressed the button on the privacy window, waiting until it was fully shut to ask, "How much do you know about my family?"

"Only the—" She pursed her lips against saying *sketchiest*. "The most rudimentary details. I know your father passed away recently. Six months ago? I'm very sorry."

He dismissed her condolence with an abbreviated jerk of his head.

"And your mother has been gone quite a bit longer?" she murmured gently.

"Twenty years. We were eleven." The flex of agony in his expression made Amy's attempts to remain impervious to him rather useless.

"That must have been a very hard loss for you and your sister. I'm so sorry."

"Thank you," he said gruffly, and something in his demeanor told her that even though his mother's death was two decades old, he still mourned her while his grief over his father was more of a worn-out fatalism.

"And Princess Sofia is…" Amy looked to her tablet, wishing she could confirm the impressions that leaped to mind. "I believe she's done some diplomatic work?" Amy had the sense it was far more substantial than a celebrity lending their name to a project.

"Sofia is extremely accomplished." His pride in his sister had him sitting straighter. "She began advocating for girls when she was one. We both studied political science and economics, but when I branched into emerging technologies, she pursued a doctorate in humanities. More recently, she played an integral part in the trade agreements in the Balkan region. She's done excellent work with refugees, maternal health and global emergency response efforts."

"I had no idea," Amy said faintly. Her parents had disinherited her and she'd come a long way from a hard start, but women like his sister made her feel like a hellacious underachiever.

"She's remarkable. Truly. And has way more patience for politics that I do. I don't suffer fools, but she's willing to take the time to bring people around to her way of thinking. We both know where Vallia needs to go, but my instinct is to drag us there through force of will. She has the temperament to build consensus and effect change at a cultural level. She's better suited to the role, is arguably more qualified and, most importantly, she's an hour older than I am. The crown should be hers by birthright."

"Wow." If her voice held a touch of growing hero worship for both of them, she couldn't help it. "It's rare to hear a powerful man sound so supportive and willing to step aside for anyone, let alone a woman. That's so nice."

"I'm not 'nice,' Amy. Shake that idea from your head right now," he said tersely. "I am intelligent enough to see what's obvious and loyal enough to my country and my sister to make the choice that is right for everyone concerned. This has nothing to do with being *nice*."

He was using that voice again, the one that seemed intent on warning her that any designs she might have on him were futile.

Message received, but that didn't stop her from lifting her chin in challenge. "What's wrong with being nice? With being kind and empathetic?"

"I'm not advocating cruelty," he said with a curl of his lips. "But those are emotions, and emotions are hungry beasts. Soon you're doing things just so you *feel* kind. So you have the outside validation of people believing you're empathetic. Ruling a country, doing it *well*—" he seemed to pause disdainfully on the word, perhaps criticizing his father's reign? "—demands that you remove your personal investment from your decisions. Otherwise, you'll do what appeases your need to feel good and lose sight of what's ethically sound."

She considered that. "It seems ironic that you believe giving up the crown is the right thing to do when your willingness to do what's right makes you ideal for wearing it."

"That's why my sister won't challenge me for it. She refuses to throw Vallia into turmoil by fighting for the right to rule, not when I'm healthy, capable and wildly popular. From an optics standpoint, she can't call me out as unsuited and install herself. She has to clearly be a better choice, recruited to save the country from another debacle."

"Why was she passed over in the first place? Primogeniture laws?"

"Sexism. Our father simply thought it would make him look weak to have a woman as his heir. He was too selfish and egotistical, too driven by base desires to see or do what was best for Vallia. When it was revealed my mother was carrying twins and that we were a boy and a girl, he declared the boy would be the next king. Even though Sofia was born first, making her the rightful successor, the council at the time was firmly in my father's pocket. No one pushed back on his decree."

"Does that council still have influence? Can't you simply abdicate?"

"I've tried." Impatience roughened his tone. "Once I was old enough to understand the reality of my position, I began to question why the crown was coming to me." He pensively tapped the armrest with a brief drum of his fingers. "Our mother knew Sofia was being cheated, but she worried that pressing for Sofia's right to inherit would cost her what little influence she had. She used her mandate of raising a future king to install a horde of conservative advisers around us. They genuinely wished to mold me into a better king than my father was, and they are extremely devoted to their cause. That isn't a bad thing, given the sort of people who surrounded my father." He side-eyed her.

Amy briefly rolled her lips inward. "I won't pretend I haven't read the headlines." Countless mistresses, for instance, sometimes more than one at a time. "I don't put a lot of stock into gossip, especially online. Paparazzi will post anything to gain clicks."

Even if Luca's father had been into polyamory, it was merely a questionable look for someone in his position, not something that negated his ability to rule.

"Whatever you've read about my father is not only true," Luca said in a dark voice, "it is the white-washed version." His voice rang as though he was hollow inside. "When he died, I brought up crowning my sister despite the fact I've always been the recognized successor. It was impressed upon me that Vallia was in too fragile a state for such a scandal. That we desperately needed to repair our reputation on the world stage and I was the man to do it."

"It's only been six months. Is Vallia strong enough

to weather you renouncing your crown?" she asked skeptically.

"It's the perfect time to demonstrate that behaviors tolerated in the previous king will not be forgiven in this one. A small, well-targeted scandal that proves my sister is willing to make the hard decision of removing me for the betterment of our country will rally the population behind her. I need something unsavory enough to cause reservations about my suitability, but not so filthy I can't go on to hold positions of authority once it's over. I don't intend to leave her in the lurch, only restore what should be rightfully hers."

"What will you do after she ascends?" she asked curiously.

"Vallia's economy has suffered from years of neglect. Recent world events have not helped. Before the duties of a monarch tied up all my time, I was focused on developing our tech sector. We have a small but exceptional team working in solar advancements and another looking at recovering plastics from the waste stream to manufacture them into useable goods."

"Be careful," she teased, noting the way his expression had altered. "You almost sound enthusiastic. I believe that's known as having an emotion."

His gaze clashed into hers. Whatever keenness might have briefly brimmed within him was firmly quashed, replaced by something icy and dangerous.

"Don't mistake my frankness for a desire to be

friends, Amy," he warned softly. "I'm giving you the information you need to do your job. You don't know me. You can't. Not just because we'll never have a shared frame of reference, but because I won't allow it. I've lived in the shadow of a man who made everything about himself. Who allowed himself to be ruled by fleeting whims and hedonistic cravings. If I thought my desire to go back to reshaping our economy offered anything more than basic satisfaction in pursuing a goal, I wouldn't do it. It's too dangerous. I won't be like him."

They were coming into a private airfield and aiming for a sleek jet that had the Vallian flag painted on the tail. A red carpet led to the steps.

Amy squirmed internally. He might not have emotions, but she did. And she was normally well-liked. It bothered her to realize he not only didn't like her, but he didn't want to. That stung. She didn't want to feel his rebuff this keenly.

"Developing a rapport with a client is a way of building trust," she said stiffly. "Given the personal nature of this work, and how I live in my client's pockets through the course of a campaign, they like to know they can trust me."

"I've paid top price for unquestionable loyalty. I don't need the frills of bond-forming banter to prove it."

Keep your mouth shut, she warned herself.

"Lucky you. It's included with every purchase," she blurted cheerfully.

The SUV came to a halt, making it feel as though his hard stare had caused the world to stop spinning and her heart to stop beating.

"Dial it back," he advised.

She desperately wanted to tell him he could use a laugh. *Lighten up*, she wanted to say, but the door opened beside her. He was the customer and the customer might not always be right, but they had to believe she thought they were.

She buttoned her lip and climbed aboard his private jet.

Did he feel regret at taking her down a notch? If Luca allowed himself emotions, perhaps he would have, but he didn't. So he sipped his drink, a Vallian liquor made from his nation's bitter oranges, and watched her through hooded eyes.

He told himself he wasn't looking for signs she'd been injured by his cut. If she was, she hid it well, smiling cheerfully at the flight attendant and quickly making a work space for herself. She made a call to her assistant to reassign various files and eschewed alcohol for coffee when offered, tapping away on her tablet the whole time.

She seemed very comfortable in his jet, which was built for comfort, but she was relaxed in the way of someone who was not particularly impressed by the luxury. As though she was familiar with such lavishness. Took it for granted.

She catered to celebrities so she had likely seen

her share of private jets. Why did the idea of her ex-
periencing some rock star's sonic boom niggle at
him, though? Who cared if she'd sat aboard a hundred yachts, allowing tycoons to eyeball her legs
until she curled them beneath her like a cat while
tracing a stylus around her lips as she studied her
tablet? It was none of Luca's business if she traded
witty barbs with stage actors or played house with
playwrights.

He was absolutely not invested in how many lovers she'd had, rich, poor or otherwise. No, he was
in a prickly mood for entirely different reasons that
he couldn't name.

He flicked the button to bring down the tempera-
ture a few degrees and loosened his tie.

"I'm sending you the contract to forward to your
legal department." Amy's gaze came up, inquiring.
Professional, with a hint of vulnerability in the tension around her eyes.

Perhaps not so unaffected after all.

A tautness invaded his abdomen. He nodded
and glanced at his phone, sending the document as
quickly as it arrived. Seconds later, he realized he
was typing her name into the search bar, planning
to look into more than her professional history. He
clicked off his phone and set it aside.

"How did you get into this type of work? The
company is only two years old, isn't it? But it won
an award recently?"

"For a multicountry launch, yes. Specifically,

'Imaginative Use of Traditional and Social Media in a Coordinated International Product Launch Campaign.'" She rolled her eyes. "These types of awards are so niche and specific they're really a public relations campaign for public relations." She shrugged. "But it's nice to have something to brag about and hopefully put us at the top of search engines for a few days."

"That's how your firm came to my attention, so it served its purpose."

"I'll let Clare know." She flashed a smile.

"Your partner." He vaguely remembered the name and photo on the website. The dark-haired woman hadn't projected the same vivacity that had reached out from Amy's headshot, compelling him to click into her bio and fall down an online wormhole of testimonials.

"Clare is one of my best friends from boarding school. London Connection was her idea. She came into some money when her father passed and wanted to open a business. I worked the social media side of things, organizing high-profile events and managing celebrity appearances. Once we were able to expand the services beyond straight promoting into problem-solving and crisis management, we exploded. We're so busy, we dragged our friend Bea from her law firm to join our team." Her face softened with affection. "We're all together again. It's the best career I could have imagined for myself."

"Boarding school," he repeated. That explained

how Amy took to private jets like a duck to water. She'd probably been raised on one of these. "I thought I detected a hint of American beneath your accent. Is that where you're from?"

"Originally." Her radiance dimmed. "We moved to the UK when I was five. I went to boarding school when my parents divorced. I was just looking up your foundation. Do I have the name right? Fondo Della Regina Vallia?"

"That's it, yes."

"I have some ideas around merchandise that would double as an awareness campaign. Let me pull a few more details together." She dipped her attention back to her tablet, corn-silk hair falling forward to curtain her face.

And that's how it was done. Replace the thing you don't want to talk about with something that seems relevant, but actually isn't.

Amy Miller was very slick and not nearly as artless and open as she wanted to appear.

Rapport goes both ways, he wanted to mock, but he didn't really want to mock her. He wanted to know her.

Who was he kidding? He wanted to know what she *liked*. She was twenty-eight, and at least a few of the men photographed with her must have been lovers. Maybe some of the women, too. What did he know? The fact was, she was one of those rare creatures—a woman in his sphere who attracted him.

His sphere was depressingly empty of viable lovers and historically well guarded against them. His mother had surrounded her children with hypervigilant tutors, mentors and bodyguards. It had been the sort of blister pack wrapping within a window box frame that allowed others to look in without touching. He and Sofia had been safely admired, but never allowed out to play.

Mostly their mother had been trying to protect her children from learning the extent of their father's profligacy, but she'd also been doing what she could for the future of Vallia. There'd been a small civil war within the palace when she died. Luca and Sofia's advisers had collided with their father's cabal— men who had had more power, but also more to hide.

In those dark days, while he and Sofia remained oblivious, deals had been struck that had kept everyone in their cold war positions. Their father's death had finally allowed Luca and his top advisers to carve the rot from the palace once and for all. Luca had installed his own people, and they all wanted to stay in the positions to which *they* had ascended— which was how he'd wound up in this predicament.

And the reason he was still living a monk's existence. He had no time and was monitored too closely to burn off sexual calories. At university, potential partners had always been vetted to the point that they'd walked away in exhausted indifference rather than run the gamut required to arrive in his bed.

As an adult moving through the hallowed halls of

world politics and visiting allied territories, he occasionally came across a woman who had as much to lose by engaging in a loose-lipped affair as he did. They would enjoy a few private, torrid nights and part ways just as quickly and quietly. The few who had progressed into a longer relationship had been suffocated by his life, by the inability to make the smallest misstep with a hemline or a break with protocol without suffering cautionary lectures from his council and intense scrutiny by the press.

Luca didn't blame women for walking out of his life the minute they saw how little room there was to move within it.

Amy would die in such a confined space. She was too bright and vivacious. It would be like putting a burning light inside a cupboard. Glints might show through the cracks, but all her heat and power would be hidden and wasted.

Why was he dreaming of crawling in there with her? Imagining it to be like closing himself within the cradle of a suntan bed, surrounded in the sweet scent of coconut oil and a warmth that penetrated to his bones.

He dragged his gaze from where the barest hint of breast swell was peeking from the open buttons of her dress and set his unfinished drink aside. Best to slow down if he was starting to fantasize about a woman he'd hired—to *ruin* him.

He bet she could ruin him. He just bet.

His assistant came to him with a tablet and a handful of inquiries, and Luca forced his mind back to who he was and the obligations he still had—for now.

Perhaps when this was over, he promised himself, he would be able to pursue the iridescent Amy. Until then, he had to remain the honorable and faultless king of Vallia.

CHAPTER THREE

AMY'S FATHER USED to joke that he had oil in his veins and a rig where his heart ought to be. His great-grandfather had hit a gusher on a dirt farm in Texas, and the family had been filling barrels with black gold ever since. Her father was currently the president of Resource Pillage International or whatever name his shell company was using these days. He had moved back to Texas shortly after the divorce, remarried, and was too busy with his new children to call his eldest more than once or twice a year.

Amy's mother came from a family of bootleggers, not that she would admit it. *Her* great-grandfather had been born when Prohibition ended. The family had quickly laundered their moonshine money into legal breweries throughout the Midwest. Two generations later, they had polished away their unsavory start with a chain of automobile showrooms, fashion boutiques, and most importantly, a Madison Avenue advertising firm.

Amy's mother had taken the quest for a better

image a step further. After pressing her husband to move them to London, she had traded in her New York accent for an upper-crust British one. Since her first divorce, she had continued to scale the social ladder by marrying and divorcing men with names like Nigel who held titles like lord chancellor.

Amy had to give credit where it was due. Her mother had taught her that if reality wasn't palatable, you only had to finesse the details to create a better one. *Of course I want you to live with me, but boarding school will expose you to people I can't.* And, *Delaying access to your trust fund isn't a punishment. It's a lesson in independence.*

People often remarked how good Amy was at her job, but she wasn't so much a natural at repackaging the truth as a lifelong victim of it. Case in point, her mother's first words when Amy answered her call were, "You wish to cancel our lunch Wednesday?"

As if Amy had been asking for permission.

Amy reiterated what she'd said in her text. "I had to run out of town. I can't make it."

"Where are you?"

In a car with the king of Vallia, winding up a series of switchbacks toward the remains of a castle that overlooked the Tyrrhenian Sea.

"I'm with a client."

"Who?"

"You know I can't tell you."

"Amy, if he won't let you talk about your relationship, it's not going anywhere." Perhaps if her mother had worked at the family firm instead of choosing "heiress" as her career, she would know that Amy's job was not a front for pursuing men with fat money clips.

"Can I call you later, Mom? We're almost at our destination."

"Don't bother. I can't make lunch, either. Neville— You remember him? He's the chargé d'affaires to Belgium. He's taking me to Australia for a few weeks."

"Ah. Lovely. Enjoy the beach."

"Mmm." Her mother sniffed disdainfully. She was more vampire than woman, eschewing sunshine in favor of large-brimmed hats and absorbing her vitamin D through high-priced supplements. "Behave yourself while I'm gone. Neville is ready to propose. I wouldn't want to put him off."

Seriously, Mom? It's been ten years. But her mother never missed an opportunity to remind her.

Amy's stomach roiled with suppressed outrage, but she only said through her teeth, "You know me, all work and no play. Can't get into trouble doing that."

"You wear short skirts to nightclubs, Amy. That sort of work is— Well, I'm sure I can persuade Neville to introduce you to someone if you manage not to mess this up for me."

Could Luca hear what her mother was saying? He'd finished his own call and pocketed his phone. This town car was the sort that made the drive feel like a lazy canal ride inside a noise-canceling bubble.

"I have to go, Mom. Travel safe." Amy cut off the call, which would result in a stinging text, but she wasn't sorry. She was hurt and angry. Bea and Clare always told her she didn't have to talk to her mother if it only upset her, but Amy lived in eternal hope that something would change.

"Everything all right?" Luca was watching her with a look that gave away nothing.

She realized she had huffed out a beleaguered sigh.

"Fine," she lied sunnily. "Mom's off to Australia."

"You didn't mention any siblings earlier. Are you an only child?"

"The proverbial spoiled kind. I had one of everything except a brother or sister, which is why my friends are so special to me. Will I meet your sister?"

There was a brief pause that made her think he knew she was deliberately turning the question around to avoid delving into her own past.

"She's traveling, due home later this week," he replied evenly.

They were driving past the shell of the castle. As they came even with a courtyard bracketed by two levels of arches in various states of disintegration, she glimpsed a young woman in a uniform leading what looked like a group of tourists. They all turned to point their phones at the car's tinted windows as it passed.

Seconds later, when they halted to wait for golden gates to crawl open, Amy glanced back, curious.

"The castle is a heritage site," Luca explained. "Open for booked tours. The island of Vallia was a favorite summer destination for Roman aristocracy. The palace is built on the remains of an emperor's villa. You'll see what's left in one of the gardens." He nodded as the palace came into view.

"Wow."

At first glance, the imposing monument to baroque architecture, ripe with columns and domes and naves, was almost too much. Amy could hardly take in everything from the serpentine balcony to the elaborate cornices to the multitude of decorative details like seashells and ribbons. Stone angels held aloft what she presumed to be Vallia's motto, carved into the facade.

"This is amazing."

"You can accomplish a lot when you don't pay for labor," Luca said, mouth twisting with resigned disgust. "Vallia was a slave trading post through the Byzantine era. Then the Normans used them to build the fortress while they were taking over southern Italy." He nodded back to the castle. "They sent the slaves into the fields to grow food, and the first king of Vallia used them again to build this palace in the late 1600s, when the Holy Roman Emperor established the kingdom of Vallia."

Despite its dark history, she was in awe. The white stone of the palace was immaculately tended and blindingly beautiful. The gardens were lush, the windows reflecting the blue skies and colorful blooms.

"It's not showing its age at all."

"My father had it fully restored and modernized."

"The workers were paid this time, I hope?" It was out before she thought better of it.

Luca's expression hardened. "A livable wage for honest employment, thanks to efforts by my sister and I, because he couldn't be dissuaded from doing it. Hardly the best use of Vallia's taxes, though."

Amy managed to bite back her observation that he didn't sound as though he had been super close with his dad.

They stepped from the car, and the comforting warmth of sunbaked stones radiated into her while a soft, salt-scented breeze rolled over her skin. The palace was set into terraced grounds facing the sea, but the view stretched east and west on either side. Flowers were bursting forth in splashes of red and yellow, his country's colors, in the gardens and in terra-cotta pots that sat on the wide steps. New leaves on the trees ruffled a subtle applause as they climbed toward the entrance.

A young man hurried to open a door for him.

Entering the palace was a step into a sumptuous garden of white marble streaked with pinks and blues, oranges and browns. Ornate plasterwork and gold filigree climbed the walls like vines, sweeping in curves and curls up to the sparkling crystal chandeliers. The fresco painted on the dome above had her catching at Luca's arm, it made her so dizzy.

Amid the cerulean skies and puffy clouds and beams
of sunlight, the angels seemed rather…sexual.

They weren't angels, she realized with a lurch of
her heart. That satyr definitely had his hand between
the legs of a nymph.

A man cleared his throat.

Amy jerked her gaze down to see a palace sage
of some type, middle-aged, in a dark suit. His gaze
was on her hand, which still clutched Luca's sleeve.

She let it fall to her side.

"Amy, this is Guillermo Bianchi, my private secretary. Guillermo, Amy Miller. She's with London
Connection, a public relations firm. She'll assist with
the foundation's gala."

"I received the email, *signor.*" Guillermo nodded
as both greeting and acknowledgment of her role.
"Welcome. Rooms have been prepared and appoint-
ments arranged with the team."

"Thank you. Er…*grazie*, I mean."

"Amy will join me for dinner in my dining room
while she's here."

Guillermo gave an obsequious bow of his head
that still managed to convey disapproval. He asked
Amy to accompany him up a wide staircase beneath
a massive window that allowed sunlight to pour in
and shoot rainbows through the dangling chandelier.

She looked back, but Luca was already disappearing in another direction toward a handful of people
waiting with tablets, folders and anxious expressions.

Amy went back to gawking at the opulence of the

palace. She'd grown up with enough wealth to recognize hand-woven silk rugs and antiques that were actually priceless historical artifacts. She lifted her feet into a slight tiptoe when they reached a parquet floor, fearful of damaging the intricate artistry of the polished wood mosaic with her sharp heels. She could have stood upon it for hours, admiring the geometric designs.

This whole place was a monument to ancient wealth and abundance that stood on the line of gaudy without quite crossing it.

After a long walk through a gallery and down a flight of stairs, she was guided into a lounge that was a perfect mix of modern and period pieces. It had a wide gas fireplace, tall windows looking onto a garden with a pond, and Victorian furniture that she suspected were loving restorations. Everything in the room was the height of class—except the pornographic scene above the sofa. Amy blinked.

"The previous king commissioned a number of reproductions from Pompeii," Guillermo informed her in bland, barely accented English. "I've ordered tea and sandwiches. They'll be here shortly. Please let the maid know if you require anything else."

Amy almost asked whether the sofa was a pullout, but he was already gone.

She poked around and discovered this was a self-contained flat with a full kitchen, a comfortable office with a view to the garden, and two bedrooms, each with more examples of Pompeii's salacious artwork.

Her meager luggage was waiting to be unpacked in the bigger room alongside a handful of clothes that were unfamiliar, but were in her size. There was a luxurious bath with a tempting, freestanding tub, but she only washed her hands.

A three-tiered plate arrived full of sandwiches, savory pastries and chocolate truffles, and was accompanied by coffee, tea and a cordial that turned out to be a tangy sweet liquor meant to be served with the soda water that accompanied it.

She did her best not to reveal she was completely bowled over, but she was only *around* wealth these days. London Connection was doing well, but they were reinvesting profits and using them to hire more staff. Amy had conditioned herself to live on a shoestring after being expelled from school. She'd been unable to take her A-levels and had had to sell what possessions she'd had at the time—mostly designer clothes and a few electronics—to set herself up in a low-end flat. She'd come a long way since then, but the maid probably had a higher net worth than she did.

Amy asked her to set the meal on the table outside her lounge. The patio overlooked a man-made pond full of water lilies where a weathered Neptune rose from the middle, trident aloft. Columns that were buckling with age surrounded the water. This must be the ruins of the Roman villa that Luca had mentioned, she thought.

Between the columns stood statues that looked new, though. Huh. The gladiator had a bare backside that rivaled Luca's, and the mermaid seemed very chesty.

After the maid left, Amy gave in to curiosity. She set aside her tea to walk out for a closer look.

"My father's taste was questionable," Luca said behind her. "To say the least."

She swung around, but had to look up to find him. He stood on a terrace off to the right that she surmised was the best vantage point to admire the pond. He wore the clothes he'd had on earlier, but his jacket was off again and his sleeves were rolled back. His expression was shuttered, but once again she heard the denigration of his father's waste of taxpayers' money.

"I thought I wouldn't see you until dinner." She had been looking forward to reflecting, putting today's events into some sort of order in her mind. Now she was back to a state of heightened awareness, watching his long strides make for a set of stairs off to the left. He loped down them and came toward her in an unhurried stride that ate up the ground easily.

"I don't want any delay on your work."

"Oh, um." Her throat had gone dry, and she looked longingly back at her tea. "I was about to sit down and brainstorm ideas, but I'm having trouble understanding why you'd willingly give up all of this." She waved at her small flat. His private quarters were likely ten times more luxurious and grand. Looking up, she suspected his was that second-level terrace that looked out to the sea unobstructed.

"Allow me to enlighten you." He jerked his head at the pebbled path that wove through the columns around the pond, indicating they should walk it.

She started along and immediately came upon a soldier performing a lewd act with a nymph, one that made her cheeks sting with embarrassment. It grew worse when she darted a glance at Luca and discovered him watching her reaction.

Her heart lurched, but he didn't seem to be enjoying her discomfiture. If anything, his grim expression darkened.

"Oh, those Romans," she joked weakly.

"My father commissioned them. He could have used the funds in a thousand better ways. My first act once I was crowned was tax relief, but I couldn't offer as much as was needed. Our economy is a mess."

Their footsteps crunched as they wound between the columns and wisteria vines that formed a bower, filling the air with their potent fragrance.

The statues grew increasingly graphic. Luca seemed immune, but Amy was as titillated as she was mortified. She was mortified *because* she was titillated.

Even more embarrassing was a stray curiosity about whether Luca would have the strength to have freestanding sex like that, arms straining as his fingertips pressed into her bottom cheeks. His shoulders would feel like marble beneath her arms where she clasped them tightly around his neck, breasts mashed to his flexing chest as her legs gripped around his waist. They would hold each other so tightly, they would barely be able to move, but—

"Do you know why Vallia needs a queen, Amy?"

"No," she squeaked, yanking her mind from fornication.

"Because the king of Vallia is this." He nodded toward the statuary. "A sex addict who never sought help. In fact, he used his position to take advantage of those over whom he had power."

The butterflies in her stomach turned to slithering snakes that crept up to constrict her lungs and tighten her throat.

Amy knew all about men who took advantage of their position of power. It was adding a razor edge of caution to every step as they walked among these erotic statues.

Luca was a client, which made her feel as though she had to defer to him, but he wasn't forcing her into an awkward situation for his own amusement. She might be blushing so hard the soles of her feet hurt, but he was radiating furious disgust. He was trying to explain why he was so committed to her doing this odd job for him.

Not that kind of job, Amy! She dragged her gaze off the woman whose hands were braced on a naked gladiator's sandals as he sat proudly feeding his erection to her.

"You're not like him," she managed to say. "Your father, I mean."

"No, I'm not," he agreed, jaw clenched. "But I have to make at least a few people believe I could be. Briefly." He glanced from the narrow shadow of the trident on a stepping-stone to his watch.

She followed his gaze and said with delight, "It's a sundial! Half-past oral sex and a quarter till—" She slapped her hand over her mouth, cheeks flaring so hotly, she thought she'd burn her palm. "I'm sorry." She was. "I use humor to defuse tension, but I shouldn't have said that. This is a professional relationship. I'll do better, I promise."

She was still stinging with a flush of embarrassment that boiled up from too many sources to count— the situation, the blatant thing she'd just said, the lack of propriety on her part and, deep down, a pang of anguish that she was giving him such a terrible impression of herself when she wished he would like her a little.

His mouth twisted. "You'll have to say a lot worse than that to shock me. The Romans themselves couldn't hold a candle to some of the obscene things my father did."

He veered down a path to a small lookout that was mostly overgrown. A wooden bench faced a low, stone wall, but they had to stand at the wall to see the blue-green water beyond.

Compassion squeezed Amy's insides as she sensed the frustration rolling off him.

"I've worked with a lot of people trying to keep scandals under wraps. It's very stressful. I can only imagine the pressure you've been under since you took the throne."

Luca made a noise that was the most blatantly cynical sound Amy had ever heard.

"For my whole life," he corrected her grimly. "As long as I can remember I've been trying to hide it, fix it, compensate for it. I've had to be completely different from him despite looking exactly like him while training for his job. A position he made seem so vile, there is absolutely no desire in me to hold it."

At his own words, he swore under his breath and ran a hand down his face.

"That sounds treasonous. Forget I said it," he muttered.

"This is a safe space. It has to be." Amy had long ago trained herself not to judge what people revealed when they were in crisis. "Are you still under pressure to hide his behavior? If there are things you're worried could come out, I might be able to help manage that, too." She looked to where the array of erotic statues was shielded by shrubbery. "I could put out confidential feelers for a private collector to buy those, for a start."

"That's well-known." He dismissed the statues with a flick of his hand. "There's no point trying to hide them now."

His jaw worked as though he was debating something. When he looked at her, a cold hand seemed to leap out of his bleak gaze and close over her heart.

"The way he died may yet come out," he admitted in a voice that held a scraped hollow ring, one that held so much pain, she suspected he was completely divorcing himself from reality to cope with it.

"Do you want to tell me about it? You don't have to," she assured him while her heart stuttered in an uneven rhythm. "But you can if you want to."

His father's death had been reported as a cardiac arrest, but there'd been countless rumors about the circumstances.

"My sister doesn't even know the full truth."

It was all on him and the secret weighed heavily. Amy could tell.

She wanted to touch him, comfort him in some way. She also sensed he needed to be self-contained right now. It was the only way he was holding on to his control.

"If you're worried there are people who might reveal something, we could approach them with a settlement and a binding nondisclosure," she suggested gently.

"That's already been done. And the handful of people who knew where he was that night were happy to take a stack of cash and get away without a charge of contributing to manslaughter, but they're not the most reliable sort." He searched her gaze with his intense one. "Frankly, I wish he'd hired prostitutes. They would have acted like professionals. This was a party gone wrong. There were drugs at the scene. Nasty ones."

"Here? In the palace?" That was bad, but she'd cleaned up similar messes.

"In the dungeon."

She didn't school her expression fast enough.

"Yes. *That* kind of dungeon." His lips were snarled tight against his teeth. His nostrils flared. "I wouldn't normally judge how people spend their spare time, but if you rule a country, perhaps don't allow yourself to be tied up and flogged by a pair of women who get so stoned they don't know how to free you when your heart stops. Or who to call."

Amy caught her gasp in her hand. Talk about making a traumatic situation even more distressing for all involved!

"Luca, I'm so sorry." Her hand went to his arm before she realized she was doing it.

He didn't react beyond stiffening under her touch.

She'd seen clients shut down like this, doing whatever they had to in order to carry on with their daily lives. It told her exactly how badly his father's behavior had affected him.

"Look, I have to ask before we go any further. Are you sure you're not just reacting to what you've experienced? I'd want to wash my hands of this role if I were in your shoes. That's understandable, but what you've asked me to do is not a decision you should make in haste."

"It's not one incident, Amy. It's everything he stood for. All of the things I've learned he was capable of, now that I'm privy to it. It's appalling. There was a thorough cleaning of house once I took the throne, but how can I claim to be righting his wrongs if I ignore the very basic one where he installed me as monarch instead of my sister?"

The flash of a tortured conscience behind his scaring blue eyes tempted her to shift her fingers in a soothing caress. She moved her hand to the soft moss that had grown on the stone wall and scanned the view through the trees.

"And no one will listen to this extremely rational argument? Let you turn things over without drastic measures?"

"My supporters see Sofia as an excellent spare, but they are extremely attached to keeping me exactly where I am. Our constitution doesn't allow an abdication without proper cause. Even if I was incapacitated, I would keep the crown and Sofia would rule as a regent until I died. I've exhausted all other avenues. This is what's left. I have to prove myself a detriment to the country. An embarrassment that can't be tolerated because I'm too much like my father after all."

"Okay. Well…" She considered all she'd learned, formally and informally. "Most scandals fall into three categories—sex, drugs and corruption. It sounds like your father had his toe in all of those?"

"He did."

"It's hard to come back from embezzlement or political payoffs. I wouldn't want to tar you as a crook, especially if you're planning to take an active part in improving Vallia's economy afterward."

"Agreed."

"Drug scandals usually require a stay in a rehab facility and ongoing counseling. Addiction is an illness, so there's a risk you'd be expected to continue to rule. It's also very complicated to manage image-wise. There has to be sincere, visible effort, and it becomes a lifelong process of proving sobriety. There's always a certain mistrust that lingers in the public eye. The world expects a recovering addict to trip and is always watching for it. I would prefer not to use a drug scandal."

"So that leaves us with sex." His mouth curled with dismay.

"Yes. People love to act outraged over sexual exploits, but they all have their own peccadillos to hide so they tend to move on fairly quickly."

"It can't be anything harassment related or exploitative," he said firmly.

"No," she quickly agreed. "I couldn't defend that, even a manufactured charge. London Connection is always on the victim's side in those cases. It will have to be something compromising, like cheating or adultery." She tapped her chin in thought.

"That would mean courting my way into a relationship with someone in order to betray her. I don't want to use or hurt an unsuspecting woman."

"Something that suggests you have a streak of your father's tastes, then?"

"I'm won't be tied up and spanked. That's not my thing."

"Like anyone would believe you're a bottom. I'm sorry!" She hid her wince behind her hand. "These are habits of a lifetime, trying to be funny to keep a mood light."

After a silence that landed like a thump, he drawled, "I'm definitely a top." The firmness in his tone underscored his preference for dominating in bed.

Which caused the most inexplicable swoop in her stomach. Runnels of tingling intrigue radiated into her loins, much to her everlasting chagrin.

When she risked a glance up at him, she saw humor glinting in his eyes along with something speculative that noted the blush on her cheekbones.

Her heart swerved, and she shot her attention to the sea while her shoulders longed for the weight of his hands. Something wanton in her imagination pictured him drawing her arms behind her back by the elbows while he kissed the side of her neck and told her not to move.

While he held her. *Claimed* her.

Her scalp tingled in anticipation and she refused to look down, deeply aware her nipples were straining against the soft silk of her dress, swollen and tight and throbbing with lust.

"Perhaps…um…" Her voice rasped and her brain

was wandering around drunk in the dark. "Something with role-play?" she suggested tautly.

"Leak a photo of me wearing pointy ears or dressed like one of those gladiators?" He thumbed back toward the path. "No, thanks."

He would so *rock* a leather sword belt. She licked her lips. "Voyeurism?"

"Hidden cameras? Gross."

"What if you, um, did something questionable in public?"

"Caught with my pants down? Like a flasher?"

"*With* someone."

"Mmm." He grimaced as he considered it. "It has potential, but it means compromising someone else, and naked photos are forever. Keep going."

"You're really hard to please."

"You'll get there," he chided.

A fluttery excitement teased through her.

"Group sex?" she suggested, then realized that might be *too* reminiscent of his father.

Luca's gaze held her own in a way that made her stumbling heart climb into her throat.

"I prefer to give one woman one hundred percent of my attention," he stated. "And I refuse to compete for hers."

So dominant.

Bam, bam, bam went her heart, hammering the base of her throat while the rest of her was slithery honey and prickly nerve endings.

"The only thing left is tickle fights and foot fe-

DANI COLLINS
63

tishes." She turned her gaze to the water, nose quest-ing for any hint of breeze to cool her blood. She was boiling inside her own skin.

"I like a pretty shoe," he allowed in a voice that angled down to where her silk dress fluttered against her ankles. His voice climbed as his attention came up. "Quality lingerie is always worth appreciating."

He could see the sea-foam green of her lacy bra cup peeking from the open buttons at her chest; she was sure of it. Could he also see she was fighting not to pant in reaction? Why, oh, why was she respond-ing to him so strongly?

"But it's hardly a crime to admire a beautiful woman, is it?"

Was that what he was doing? Because she was pretty sure she was being seduced.

"I want to do something *bad*, Amy."

She choked on a semihysterical laugh, fighting to stay professional and on task while imagining him— *Don't*, she scolded herself. *Don't imagine him doing anything, especially not making babies with y—*

"Oh! Baby daddy!" She leaped on it, pointing so hard toward him, she almost poked him in the chest. "A woman claims to be pregnant with your baby."

His brow went up toward his hairline. "That sort of extortion died when DNA tests came along, didn't it?"

"That's why it would be taken seriously." She spoke fast as she warmed to it. "Women don't make the claim unless they've actually slept with the potential father. Here's what I like about this idea." She excitedly ticked off on her fingers. "It's a very human mistake that still makes you seem virile, and you'll take the honorable steps to accept responsibility. But, because she's not suitable as a queen, it opens the door for your sister to question your judgment and take over."

"It won't work." He dismissed it flatly. "If I conceive a baby while I'm on the throne, my honor would demand that I marry her. That child would become the future ruler of Vallia and my sister would be sidelined forever."

"There is no baby." Amy opened her hands like it was a magic act. "We'll keep the timeline very short. We leak that a woman approached you and *thinks* she's pregnant. You take the possibility seriously, but even while the scandal is blowing up, she learns it was a false alarm. She wasn't actually pregnant. That way the trauma of a pregnancy loss can be avoided. The scandal will be about you taking reckless chances with your country's future. Your sister can call you irresponsible and take the throne."

His brow was still furrowed. "There's no actual woman? I'm the only name in the press? I like that."

"I think you need a living, breathing woman." She wrinkled her nose. "Otherwise the public will search forever for this mystery woman. You'd have people coming forward for generations, claiming to be your long-lost descendant. No, you need someone you conceivably—ha-ha—could have met and slept with. Perhaps a reality star or a pop singer. Let me go through my contact list. I'm sure I can find a few women who would be willing to do something like this as a publicity stunt."

He cringed.

"You hate it?" She had been so proud, convinced this was a workable plan.

"I don't love that I have to use someone, but if she's in the know from the beginning and getting something out of it, I can live with it. This sounds effective without being too unsavory." He nodded. "Run with it."

CHAPTER FOUR

A DISTANT NOISE INTRUDED, but Luca ignored it and continued indulging his lascivious fantasy of Amy's dress unbuttoned to her waist, held closed only by the wide black corset-style belt. Her lacy green bra and underwear would hold the heat of her body and have a delicious silky abrasive texture against his lips and questing touch. She—

"Signor?" His private secretary and lifelong adviser cleared his throat very pointedly, forcing Luca to abandon his musing and focus on the fact that Guillermo was standing in his office, awaiting acknowledgment.

"Yes?" Luca prompted.

"About Ms. Miller's work with the charity…" Guillermo closed the door.

"Is she shaking things up? Because that's what I hired her to do." If she appeared to be an impulsive, misguided decision on his part, all the better.

Guillermo's mouth tightened before he forced a flat smile. "The palace PR team is perfectly capable of handling this last-minute promotion of the gala. In fact, the foundation's board could carry the event over the finish line without any help at all so I'm not sure why Ms. Miller is necessary."

This was the sort of micromanaging Luca had suffered all his life and would have burned to the ground if he'd been planning to remain king. Given their lifelong relationship, Luca could also tell Guillermo smelled an ulterior motive and was digging to find it.

"The board of directors are my mother's contemporaries," Luca said. "They're committed and passionate, but at some point, adhering to tradition only demonstrates a lack of imagination. We're there."

"Have you seen Ms. Miller's contemporaries? Her online presence is very colorful." It wasn't a compliment.

"She's well-connected and understands how to leverage that community."

"But to *whom* is she connected, *signor*? That is my concern. She's photographed with a lot of men, often in relation to a drug charge or the like."

"It's her job to mitigate scandals."

"Are we certain she's not actually the source of them?" Guillermo wasn't being an alarmist. Their previous head of PR had been an enabler to the former king's vices. "Even if she's aboveboard, she wishes to pitch the directors on having the foundation's logo embroidered onto pajamas to be sold as a fundraiser. She thinks celebrities could be encouraged to post photos of themselves wearing them.

Might I remind you, *signor*, of your standing instruction that all those associated with royal interests project a more dignified profile than we've seen in the past? Have I missed an announcement that your attitude has changed?"

"You know it hasn't," Luca said flatly. "I'll have Amy tell me about the pajama idea over dinner and judge for myself."

Guillermo didn't take the hint that he was dismissed. "Is dining with her a good idea? She's very familiar. She makes frequent jokes."

Dio aiutami, his patience was hanging by a thread. "Off with her head, then."

"I'm merely pointing out that if she were a true British subject, she might understand the role of a sovereign, but she was born in America—"

"She has the gall to be an American? What *will* we do?"

"*Signor*, I wouldn't want her levity or imprudence to cast any shadows upon you."

"A moment ago, she was too colorful. Would she not cast rainbows?"

"She is already rubbing off on you if you're not taking my counsel seriously. Ms. Miller is a poor fit for any palace endeavor," Guillermo insisted.

"On the contrary, Amy understands influence and image better than you or I ever will. That's why I hired her." Luca was genuinely annoyed by his secretary's snobbish dismissal of a woman who was a font of problem-solving ideas. She had quickly grasped the pros and cons of his unusual request and shaped a workable plan in the shortest possible time. She was the type of person he loved to hire. Instead, he was surrounded by stodgy relics who started their day by shooting protocol directly into their veins.

"I'm sure her *image* is what influenced you," Guillermo sniffed.

"What are you implying?" Luca narrowed his eyes.

"Only that she's very beautiful. The sort of woman who might charm and distract a man from his duties. Impact his judgment."

"I hadn't noticed," Luca lied flagrantly, adding with significant bite, "But if you're having trouble seeing past the fact she's attractive, I'll work with her personally. Safer for all."

"*Signor*, I am perfectly capable of working with her."

"But I'm not?" Luca was down to his last nerve. "I am thirty-one and the king. It's time you trust me to know what I'm doing." *As I nuke my own life... but needs must.*

Do you? Guillermo didn't say it, but the words echoed around the room all the same.

"You're dismissed."

Guillermo closed the door on his way out with a firm click.

Luca hissed out a disgusted breath. Guillermo wasn't stupid. Or wrong. If he'd been a true detriment to the family, the palace, or Vallia, he wouldn't hold the position he did.

Luca was resolved, however, in giving up the crown. The part where he was all too aware of Amy's attributes wasn't part of the plan. He was crossing certain lines if only within his own mind, imagining how snugly silk and lace would sit against Amy's skin. It reinforced temptations that were already difficult to resist.

And much as he was willing to appear fallible, he didn't want to do anything that would sit on his conscience—like make an unwanted pass at an employee. Dignity and responsibility had been his watchwords all his life. He had never had room for even those small human mistakes that Amy found so forgivable.

Her accepting nature was as disarming as her sense of humor and sparkling beauty. He'd signed the contract she'd sent him so he knew she was legally bound to keep his secrets, but he was still unnerved at how easily he'd told her about his father. The night of his father's death had been horrific and something he'd expected to take to his grave—even though it sat inside him like a boil.

Lancing that poison had been a profound relief. Maybe she was onto something about building rapport with her clients.

He choked on a fresh laugh as he recalled her blurted joke. *Half-past oral sex and quarter till—*

What had she been about to say? Doggy-style?

So inappropriate, considering their professional relationship, but damned if he wouldn't recall that remark every time he looked at the sundial in future. And laugh instead of wanting to bash it apart with a sledgehammer.

He'd fought noticing how the graphic statues were affecting her as they walked through them. She'd been curious, as anyone would be. They were meant to be sexually provocative. He'd seen her blushes and lingering looks and the way her nipples had poked against the cups of her bra beneath the layer of her silk dress.

He'd had his own stiffness to disguise. In another life they might have had an entirely different sort of conversation among those athletic examples of libidinous acts, one that might have ended in an attempt to emulate—

Stop. He couldn't let himself do this. He had *hired* her.

To ruin him.

And their conversation on how best to go about that had been some of the most amusing banter he'd enjoyed in ages.

Guillermo was right. Amy could be very dangerous to him on a personal level.

Even so, he glanced at his watch and decided he was hungry for an early dinner.

Amy eyed the slim-fit chive-green pants and the madras patterned jacket in pink and green and gold that she'd bought from the hotel boutique. They would work for tomorrow's meeting with Luca's gala committee, but it wasn't a formal enough outfit for dining with a king.

She debated between the two tea dresses in the closet. One was a pale rose, the other a midnight blue. Both were exceedingly good quality, elegant and pretty, but so demure as to bore her into a coma while looking at them. That pastel pink with the long sleeves would make her skin look sallow, and its sweetheart neckline would have her begging for an insulin shot.

She tried on the blue. It had a round collar, cap sleeves and a sheer overlay on the A-line skirt. She was tempted to put her own leather corset belt over it, but tried the belt off the pink dress. It was a narrow plait with a spangled clasp that added some pop against the blue.

She ignored the closed-toe black patent leather pumps and put on her own silver-heeled stilettos. Then she pushed all her bangles so they sat above her elbow. She couldn't hide the tattoo on her upper arm and shoulder, so she underscored it.

Her hair was in a topknot with wisps pulled out at her temples. Simple eye makeup made her new crimson lipstick all the more dramatic. She was ready to face Luca.

She hoped.

The young man who escorted her—was he a footman?—glanced at her in the various reflective surfaces they passed. She wasn't falsely modest. She knew she attracted the male gaze. Even before her curves had developed, her mother had coached her to play up her femininity and keep the men around her happy and comfortable.

Manipulate them, was what her mother had meant. Trouble was, she'd taught Amy to hunt without teaching her to kill. Thus, Amy's first experience had been to successfully stalk a predator and become his prey without even realizing what was happening.

But she wouldn't think about that right now. The footman was letting her into an office that held a small lounge area and a scrumptious king.

"Amy," Luca greeted.

The impact of his presence, of a voice that sounded pleased to see her, was a blast of sensual energy that made all the hair on her body stand up.

He was freshly shaved and wore dark pants with a pale blue shirt. Both were tailored to sit flawlessly against his muscled frame. Funny how she almost wished he wore a jacket and tie so this would feel more formal. She wasn't sure why she wanted him to put up armor against her, but it would have made her feel safer.

Not that she felt *un*safe as the door closed, leaving them alone. She just wanted him to put up barriers because she couldn't find any of her own. She suddenly felt very raw and skinless as she faced him.

So she turned her attention to the old-world decor, the fine rugs and carved wooden columns. No overtly sexual images in here. It was decorated in a combination of modern abstracts, contemporary furniture and a few period pieces. His desk had to be three hundred years old. It was all very beautiful and…impersonal.

He hadn't moved in. Not properly. He might have erased his father's presence, but he'd made no effort to stamp the space with his own. He'd been planning his abdication from the day he was crowned.

When she looked at him, she caught him staring at her tattoo.

"You really don't care for convention, do you?" he said.

Her toes tried to curl, reacting to the conflicting mix of approval in his tone with the suggestion of disapproval in his words.

"Does that bother you?" she asked, voice strained by the pressure in her chest.

"Some." He poured two glasses of white wine and brought them across the room to offer one. "This is our private reserve. If you don't care for it, I have a red that's not as dry."

"I'm sure it will be fine." She accepted it, and they touched the rims of their glasses before she tried the wine. It was icy and very dry, but complex with a fruit forward start, a round mouth feel and a brief tang before its soft finish. "This is lovely. I'll take payment in cases."

His mouth twitched. He nodded at her shoulder. "Do you mind? I saw online that you had one, but I didn't see what it was."

She angled slightly so he could examine the inked image of a bird flying free of a cage suspended from a branch of blossoms.

"Colorful," he murmured. Something in his amused tone was drier than the wine. It made her feel as though he was making a joke she didn't understand, but his thumb grazed her skin, blanking her mind while filling her body with heat. "It must have taken a lot of time."

"Four hours. It hurt so much," she said with a laugh that was shredded more by her longing for another caress than any memory of pain. "It's too on-the-nose and was a foolish expense since I was broke at the time, but my mother had always threatened to disinherit me if I got a tattoo. Since she'd gone ahead and done that, I saw no reason to wait."

"The same mother you spoke with in the car today? The one who spoiled you because you were an only child?"

"Yes. But then she stopped." She wrinkled her nose. "I'd rather not talk about my parents. It's a complicated relationship."

"That's fine," he said mildly. "But you *can* talk about them if you decide you'd like to. This is a safe space," he added in a sardonic tone that threw her own words back at her.

She choked back saying it didn't feel like it and said, "Good to know." She gulped wine to wet her dry throat. "Do you have any?"

"Tattoos?" He snorted. "No." He sipped his own

wine, then walked his glass to an end table and set it down. "I was also forbidden to get one, but that didn't bother me. I've never had much appetite for rebellion. My father thought being king gave him license to do whatever the hell he wanted despite the responsibilities that come with the title. I was taught differently."

"By your mother and her team."

"Yes. And his behavior impacted her. She had mental health struggles. That's why the foundation exists. She started it because she understood the hurdles people face when seeking treatment. She passed away from an unrelated condition, but I often think her depression affected her…" Agony tightened his expression. "Her will to fight. She loved us, but she was very disillusioned. Humiliated by my father's conduct. Or lack thereof," he said with a twist of his lips. "He was completely indifferent to the effect he had on her. Not oblivious. He simply didn't care. If anything, he was spiteful about it. He didn't *want* to be a good husband or father or ruler. He set out to prove he didn't have to conform or put anyone's needs above his own. As a result, I find rebellion a selfish and unattractive behavior."

"Ouch," she said blithely as she set aside her own wine, fighting not to let him see how deeply that knife had plunged.

"I didn't mean to suggest you're selfish. I was speaking of the characteristic in general."

"Oh, but I was," she assured him. "I was a self-

involved brat until such time as that luxury was de-
nied me." She'd been hurt and feeling abandoned by
her parents after they'd divorced and shuffled her off
to boarding school. She'd made demands for things
she didn't even want in a clichéd cry for the love and
attention she really craved.

Her behavior had spiraled from there and yes,
Amy carried some of the blame for what had happened with the field hockey coach. She had known
what she was doing was wrong, but so had he. And
he'd been a man of twenty-nine while she'd been an
eighteen-year-old student in his class.

"I didn't always direct my independent streak in
the best way," she admitted. "But it annoys me that
pushing back on how girls and women are 'supposed
to' behave is considered rebellion. That's what I was
really fighting. My mother was always saying, 'Don't
speak up. You have to fit in.' She buys into this silent agreement with society that women aren't supposed to draw attention to ourselves because it pulls
the spotlight from the really important people. Men,"
she stated with a scathing eye roll.

"Ouch," he said ironically.

She bit her lip, quelling her smile.

He was shaking his head, but taking her remark
with good-natured amusement.

She liked him, damn it.

Best to focus on why she was here. "Can I show
you the women I've identified who might be willing to ruin you?"

"I thought I was already looking at her," he drawled.

Amy faltered in retrieving her phone.

He sobered. "That was a joke."

"I know. I didn't realize you knew how to make one." She shakily breezed past her tiny betrayal of a guilty conscience and brought her phone to him. "These are celebrities I know well enough to approach. I am neither confirming nor denying they are clients."

"Noted."

They stood so closely, she could feel the heat off his body and detected the mellow scent of his aftershave. He picked up his wine and she heard him swallow as she began to thumb through images, providing a brief biography for each.

"German car heiress trying to start her own fashion line. Country music star, American, won an award for a song about her messy divorce. This is a cousin of a British ambassador. She has a popular online cooking series."

Luca rejected them all just as quickly. "Too young. No one will believe I listen to American country music. Where would I have met an online chef?"

Six more went by and Amy clicked off her phone. "You're being too picky. *No one* will be perfect. That's the point."

"If I don't believe I'm attracted to her, no one else will." He set aside his glass again.

"What kind of woman do you want, then?" she asked with exasperation.

His gaze raked down her face and snagged on her mouth, then swept back to her eyes. The heat in the depths of his blue irises nearly set her on fire before he looked to a corner.

Amy caught her breath, swaying on the skinny heels of her shoes. She had really hoped this attraction was only on her side. It would have made this a silly infatuation where she was reaching out of her league and had no chance.

It was a lot harder to ignore when she knew he felt the same. The space between them seemed to shrink, drawing them in. Her gaze fixated on the tension around his mouth.

"I..." She had no words. She should have moved away. "I thought you were..." She thought back to that dismissive rebuff he'd given her in London. "Indifferent to me."

His lips parted as he exhaled roughly. "You do speak your mind, don't you? I *want* to be indifferent." The air crackled between them. "But I'm not."

What was she supposed to do with that? She could only soften with helplessness. He had to be the strong one.

As they both fell silent, she felt the pull of an invisible force. He moved in such small increments, she thought she imagined that he was drawing closer; but he was suddenly so close that a prickle of anticipation stung her lips. She dampened them with her tongue.

"Amy." It was a scold that rang with defeat. His hand found her hip as though to ground them both as his head dipped and he covered her mouth with his own.

Sensation burst to life in her. His lips were firm and smooth and confident. Smothering in the most delicious way as he angled and fit and claimed her. Devastated her.

How long had it been since she'd kissed a man? Really kissed one with hunger and passion and a hand that went to the back of his head, urging him to ravish her?

His arm banded across her lower back, dragging her in so her body was plastered to the hardness of his. They rocked their mouths together, pressing tighter, opening wider, exploring deeper.

A moan left her throat and she wound her arms around his neck, clinging weakly as she lost herself to the delirium. No one had ever made her feel like this. Never, ever.

Suddenly he took her by the shoulders and set her back a step. The regressive light in his eyes stopped her heart before he ruthlessly leashed whatever animal was alive inside him.

His hands dropped away as he turned to stand directly in front of her.

"Sì," he barked and the door opened.

Oh, God. Someone had knocked and she hadn't even heard it. She dropped her face into her hands.

She recognized Guillermo's voice, but stayed exactly where she was, hidden by the wall of Luca's back as she tried to gather her composure.

The men exchanged words in crisp Italian and the door closed again.

"There's a call I must take." Luca's arm reached past her to snag his wine. She heard him finish it in one gulp. "I'll be tied up for hours. Your meal will be delivered to your room."

She nodded jerkily and made herself lift her head and turn to face him. She cringed as she saw him, saying remorsefully, "My lipstick is all over your mouth."

He swore and swiped the back of his hand across his lips, noted the streak of red and swore again, this time with resignation.

"I shouldn't have done that. I'm sorry." A muscle in his cheek ticked.

Her stomach clenched around the pang his regret caused her.

"I know better, too." Her voice rasped and the backs of her eyes were hot. "I'll go."

"Amy."

She turned back.

Compunction was still etched across his face, but he held out a handkerchief. He touched her chin, urging her to lift her mouth. In a few gentle swipes, he cleaned the edges of her lips.

He then used the same soft linen to wipe his own mouth. He dropped his hand and let her examine his work. All trace of their kiss was gone as though it had never happened.

She nodded, too empty to feel anything but despondency. She swallowed a dry lump from the back of her throat, turned and left.

CHAPTER FIVE

LUCA TOOK THE CALL regarding a handful of Vallia's elite military serving overseas on a humanitarian mission. No one had been injured, but there'd been an incident that required he draft a statement and follow up with calls to overseas contacts.

By the time the whole thing was put to bed, it was long past time he should have been asleep himself.

"Take the morning off," he told Guillermo as he rose from his desk.

"Signor." Guillermo had an uncanny ability to inject a host of meaning into that single word. This one held appreciation for the sentiment, protest that the extra sleep wasn't necessary, caution and concern and a waft of smugness that he'd been right to warn Luca against Ms. Miller.

"I'll speak to the Privy Council in the morning," Luca said, meeting Guillermo's gaze with an implacable one. "You needn't make any reports to them on this evening. At all."

Guillermo's mouth tightened. "As you wish. Sleep well."

Luca didn't. He got slightly drunk while roundly berating himself even as he stood on the terrace off his bedroom, overlooking the Roman pond surrounded by sexual gymnastics.

If Amy had been wandering around there like a lost ghost, he would have had a reason to go out to see her, but she hadn't given him one.

Kissing her had been such a stupid thing to do. A mistake. Mistakes were something else he'd never had the appetite for. He'd been so scrutinized all his life, so quickly corrected for the tiniest errors, he had little tolerance for imperfection, especially within himself. He was the Golden Prince, after all.

And Amy was…

The image of her tattoo came into his mind, oddly pretty and feminine despite the jailbreak it depicted. He had wanted to clasp his hand around her warm arm and set his mouth against the ink. Taste her skin and kiss that small, pretty bird that he instinctively knew had been as chirpy inside that cage as she was outside it.

What kind of woman do you like, then?

Not anyone like her—with her cheeky remarks and hair that looked like it had already been mussed by raunchy sex. Not someone who didn't so much get under his skin as draw him out of his own. One who made him want to shake off his restraints, self-imposed and otherwise.

One with whom he'd already broken a cardinal rule of keeping his hands to himself.

He managed to sleep a few hours, then got an early start on his day. He met with his Privy Council, spoke briefly with his sister who was distracted as she wrapped up a diplomacy conference in North Africa, then made his way to the meeting of the gala committee.

Amy was holding court and faltered when he entered. She was like a tropical bird in pinks and greens and gold. Beautiful, if projecting an air of delicacy that he hadn't expected. There were hints of shadows beneath her makeup and a wary fragility in her smile.

"Your Highness," she greeted.

"Continue," he said, waving everyone to stay seated while he remained on his feet at the back of the room. "I want to hear your pitch on the pajamas."

"I'm almost there." She glanced at her slide presentation and finished talking about the recruitment of influencers. She switched to photographs of elegant satin pajamas.

"Sometimes we want to call in sick to life." Her apprehensive gaze flicked to him and her laser pointer wasn't quite steady as she circled the pajama shirt. "Sometimes we need to feel safe and cozy as we navigate personal challenges. Asking celebrities to model the foundation's merchandise isn't about making mental health struggles seem glamorous. Yes, it's a fundraiser and some people will be motivated to buy the pajamas because of who wore it best, but we're also promoting self-care. We're saying it's okay to have a pajama day."

Amy paused for reaction, seeming to hold her breath.

Heads turned to gauge his reaction. One voice said pithily, "There's no way to have them printed before the gala."

"No," Amy agreed. "The campaign would be announced at the gala with an opportunity for those attending to place preorders. People love to be on the ground floor of something new. When they received their pajamas, it would bring the foundation back to their minds. In a few months, you could offer a new color and send out reorder forms. Later in the year, you could host a low-key pajama party."

"*That* doesn't sound very dignified," someone murmured.

"I like the central message," Luca stated firmly. "And it offers flexibility moving forward. My vote is to go ahead. Amy, I'd like to meet with you on another matter when you've finished here."

The attitude in the room changed as Luca left. A few old guard on the council were sitting as though perched on a pin, but they were the type who didn't like change. The rest had been hiding their interest for fear of offending them. Now that Luca had granted royal assent, several people had excited questions and seemed eager to carry the campaign forward.

Amy contributed as best she could, but she was having trouble concentrating. She'd nearly fainted when Luca walked in. She had half expected him to announce she was off the case and should catch the first flight back to London. Last night had been a rough one full of self-recriminations—and not just because their kiss had been so improper.

Was it, though?

Or was she searching for a way to rationalize her own poor judgment?

She wasn't an impressionable student any longer. She was an adult and their kiss had been completely consensual, but Luca did have power over her, most of it financial. He also had enough influence politically and socially to destroy London Connection if he wanted to call her out as offering sex to entice his business or some other twist of the truth.

Was it naive of her to believe he would never do such a thing? She barely knew him, but she didn't believe that he had it in him to act so dishonorably.

No, the real power Luca wielded was his ability to make her cast aside common sense.

As she'd ruminated alone last night, over a meal she'd barely touched, part of her had been tempted to tear up their contract, pack up and disappear in the dead of night.

It would cost her a nonperformance fee and impact her own reputation as dedicated and reliable, but Amy had suffered through hard times before. She wasn't as vulnerable and cushioned from reality as she'd been when she'd first been expelled, either. She didn't *want* to start over, but she knew how to do it. And she had modest savings set aside for exactly the sort of emergency that would arise if she turned her back on Luca as a client.

Amy wasn't a quitter, though. And she didn't want to believe she was so weak she could fall under a man's spell and ruin her own life in the process. Not again.

Eventually, to quiet her mind, she had gone back to working on the gala presentation and the other, private assignment. If Luca decided to fire her for lacking professionalism, so be it. She, at least, would carry on as if she still had the job.

Which, it turned out, wasn't any easier than being fired. It meant facing him again. In front of a crowd. She had tried to sound knowledgeable and unaffected by the memory of their kiss while her ideas were picked apart and his laser-like gaze watched her every move.

Now the meeting had broken up and a footman was leading her back to the private wing of the palace. He showed her into a different room from last night, this one a parlor in colors of olive and straw and pale, earthy reds.

"The king will be with you shortly," he said before he evaporated.

Amy took a cleansing breath and allowed the open doors to draw her out to a small, shaded courtyard. It was full of blooming roses exuding fragrances of lemon and raspberry, green tea, honey and cloves. She felt like a bee, incapable of deciding which to sniff first.

A small round table was set with snow-white linens and a splendiferous table setting fit for—well. Duh.

She studied the gold pattern on the china plates and the scrolls of what had to be real gold applied to the glasses. A yellow orchid blossom sat on the gold napkin ring. The flatware was gold, too. Intricately patterned and heavy and engraved with the Italian word for—

"Caught you," Luca said, startling her into clattering the gold knife back into its spot.

She sent him an admonishing look while his mouth curled into an amused smirk.

He was so effortlessly perfect. Lean and athletic, confident in his own skin, moving as an intrinsic part of the beauty and luxury that surrounded him.

"I was trying to make out what it said," she grumbled. "My Italian needs work."

"The setting was commissioned for my grandparents' wedding by my great-grandmother." He touched different pieces of cutlery as he translated the various words etched upon each. "Respect, honesty, trust, loyalty. The foundation of a strong marriage."

Don't read anything into it, Amy ordered herself, but couldn't help the way her pulse quickened and her cheeks grew warm with self-consciousness.

"My grandmother always used it when she had private luncheons with her women friends." He touched a fork to minutely adjust its position. "So did my mother."

"What a lovely tradition." Her heart twisted as she

realized she was being very firmly friend zoned. "It puts a literal spin on women coming together to dish the dirt, doesn't it? I'm honored you would share it with me."

"I'm sure it made the women feel privileged to hear palace gossip from the queen herself, but if we're being honest?" He gave the knife with *Lealtà* scrolled upon it a sardonic nod. "I think it was also a reminder that the secrets she revealed were meant to be kept."

"The qualities of any good relationship, then." Amy spoke with casual interest, but her veins stung with indignation. She wasn't going to tell anyone that they'd kissed, if that's what he was worried about. "I've signed a nondisclosure contract," she reminded him, chin coming up a notch. "You don't have to drive it home with a golden spike."

"I thought you'd think they were pretty," he said in a blithe tone that disconcerted her because why would he care what she thought about anything? "The dishes and the courtyard."

"They are," she allowed, feeling awkward now. Privileged and entrusted.

He nodded past her and staff approached to seat them. Wine was poured, and as they took their first sips, her gaze clashed with his over their glasses. His expression was inscrutable, but the impact of looking him in the eye caused her to rattle the rim of her glass against her teeth. Her throat contracted on the wine, so she choked a bit, which she tried to suppress. The burn of alcohol seared a path behind her sternum.

An antipasto course was served. The staff didn't leave so they spoke of general things. Luca asked about the rest of her presentation, and Amy managed to say something lucid.

"What drew you to public relations as a career?" he inquired.

"Dumb luck. I was serving drinks at a pub. They had a band coming in, and I put it on my social media feeds. My circle was quite posh from school, daughters of celebs and such. One was a girl from a movie that was a cult favorite. She came out, and it turned the pub into that summer's hot spot. Another pub asked me to put them on the map, and word got out on the music circuit. Instead of serving drinks, I started planning and promoting events. The more people I knew, the more I got to know."

"I presumed you'd taken a degree, not learned on the job."

"I've since taken a vocational qualification." She didn't have to elaborate on why she hadn't gone to uni. Rice and fish were served, delicately spiced with saffron and scallions.

While they enjoyed it, he told her some more history about the palace and his country.

By the time they'd finished with a custard tart topped with whipped cream and fresh berries, they had discovered they both enjoyed mind-teaser puzzles, horseback riding—though they found little time to pursue it—and shared a fascination with remote places on Earth.

Amy had forgotten who he was and why she was here. This had become the most effortless, enjoyable date she'd been on in ages.

Then Luca told the server, "We'll take coffee in my drawing room," and Amy crashed back to reality. This wasn't a date.

She found a smile and said, "Coffee sounds good."

A few minutes later, they walked down the hall to the room where they'd kissed last night. The drapes were open, allowing sunshine to pour into the expansive space, but it still felt intimate once the espresso had been served and they were alone.

She understood the expression "walking on eggshells" as she approached the sofa. Each step crushed something fragile underfoot. Should she acknowledge last night? Express regret and move on? Ignore it completely and see if he brought it up?

"I saw your press release this morning," she said, deciding on an oblique reference to the phone call that had pulled them apart last night. "I'm glad things weren't more serious."

After a brief pause, he drawled, "You ought to defuse bombs for a living."

"I do," she replied mildly, obeying his wave and sinking onto the cushion. "Proverbial ones." She felt as though a sizzling string was running toward a bundle of dynamite sitting beneath her.

She added a few grains of raw, golden sugar to her coffee. He took his black.

"It's fine if we're not going to talk about it," she said in the most unconcerned tone she could find, sitting back and bringing her cup and saucer with her. "I respect boundaries. Yesterday's evidence to the contrary," she added with a wince of self-recrimination. "I don't make a habit of behaving so unprofessionally."

"My behavior was wildly inappropriate, given my title and the fact I've hired you. I want to be clear that I expect nothing from you beyond the work I've commissioned from London Connection. If our contract is something you'd prefer to dissolve now, I would understand."

Weren't they the most civilized people on the planet? And why did it make her feel as though she was swallowing acid?

"We bear equal responsibility."

"Do we?" He sounded so lethal, it struck her as an accusation. Her heart lurched.

"I'm not a victim." Conviction rang in her tone. She refused to be one ever again. "I don't think you are, either. Are you?" It took everything in her to hold his gaze and not shake so hard she'd spill hot coffee on her knee.

"No. On the contrary, I can have nearly anything I want." He smiled flatly. "It's up to me to exercise control and not take it."

"You didn't take anything I wasn't giving. I'm

not afraid to tell you no, Luca. I've done it before, I can do it again." *If I want to*. The problem was, she didn't really want to.

His expression shifted into something close to a smile, but his exhalation gave away his annoyance.

"What?" she asked caustically.

"It makes you even more attractive," he said bluntly. "That toughness inside that angelic persona you project. I find it infinitely fascinating. Which I shouldn't tell you, but we're past pretending we're not attracted to each other. Better to name the beast."

Was it? Because something ballooned in her chest, cutting off her airways. She really was going to freak out and spill hot coffee all over herself.

"It's not like we can do anything about it," she reminded him. "You're about to publicly tie yourself to another woman."

His expression shuttered, and he didn't sound pleased as he said, "True."

"I think I've found a good fit." Amy forced herself to plow forward.

"Oh?" Luca sat back, projecting skepticism. Reluctance, perhaps?

"She's an actor." She leaned forward to set her coffee on the table. "She plays a spy on that cold war series that's streaming right now. Even if you haven't seen it, people would believe you might have. It's very popular, and they film all over Europe so it's feasible you would have been in the same city at some point. We could say you were introduced by a mutual acquaintance who remains nameless. She's very pretty." Amy flicked through her phone for the woman's image.

Luca took the phone long enough to glance at it before handing it back. "Why didn't you suggest her yesterday?"

Amy almost said, *Because she's very pretty.*

"I don't know her that well. We met at a club a few weeks ago." Amy had provided a shoulder while the woman poured her heart out over a man she was having trouble quitting. "I reached out last night with a very superficial mention of a potential 'unique opportunity.' She said she'd take a meeting. I'm waiting to hear where and when."

"How much do you think she would want?"

"That's why I think she would be a good fit. Obviously, she should be compensated, but I don't think she'll care about money or publicity. She generates plenty of both on her own. But when we met, she said something that leads me to think she would find it useful to be seen as being committed to a man of your caliber."

His brows went up in a silent demand for more info.

"Romantic troubles. I don't want to gossip out of turn. I'm sure she would be more forthcoming if you formed a liaison."

He hitched his trousers as he crossed one leg over the other, looking toward the windows with a flinty expression.

Amy bit her lip, well practiced in giving a client time to process her suggestions. In this case exercising patience was especially hard. She was eager to please, but was so aware of their kiss—their mutual attraction—that it twisted her insides to suggest he even pretend to see another woman.

After a long minute, he said, "I hate this."

Her heart lurched.

Did he hate that he was sabotaging his own reputation? Or that he'd behaved badly with her and the repercussions were still coloring their discussion?

Or was he harboring a secret regret, the way she was, that they had to relegate their kiss and any potential relationship firmly offstage?

"I have to do this," he said, bringing his gaze back to hers in an ice-blue swing of a scythe. "You understand that? I don't have a choice to put it off or…" His hand scrolled the air and it sent an invisible lasso looping around her, strangling her. "I can't chase what I want at the expense of what is right. I couldn't even offer you— It would be *once*, Amy. Nothing more. And the window for that is already closing."

Amy supposed his words were a compliment, but they slapped like a rejection. Through the fiery agony, she reminded herself that she was respecting boundaries and nodded acceptance. "Don't worry about me. My job comes first."

"Same." His mouth twisted in dismay. "She sounds like a good option. Meet with her. Keep my name out of it until we're further along."

"Of course." She ignored how heavy it made her feel. "I'll have her sign confidentiality agreements before I pitch it, and I'll gauge better whether she's a good fit before you're mentioned at all."

"When will you see her?"

"I've asked for tomorrow afternoon." Her heart was pounding so hard, her ears hurt. "Do you want a slower rollout? If she turns it down, we'll have to find someone else."

"I want my sister installed as quickly as possible," he said decisively, rising.

"I think we're on the right track." She rose too, getting the message that this meeting was over. "I'll finish up my gala work while I wait to hear."

He nodded and she started to leave.

"Amy," he growled, sounding so deadly, her breath caught.

She swung around.

He wore a look of supreme frustration. His hands were in his pockets, but were fisted into rocks.

"It would only be once," he repeated grittily.

Such a bright light exploded within her, she was ignited by the heat of a thousand suns.

"Once is better than never." She ran into his arms.

CHAPTER SIX

He caught her, barely rocking on his feet. His arms wrapped tightly around her, holding her steady even as he hesitated. His lips peeled back against his teeth in a moment of strained conscience.

"It's just once," Amy blurted in a bleak urgency that awakened old ghosts inside her. The wraiths slipped and swirled in cool trails of guilt, hissing, *You shouldn't. You know you shouldn't. Nothing good will come of this.*

"Just once," he echoed in groaning agreement as he claimed her mouth with his own.

She'd been in a state of deprivation since last night. Relief poured through her as he dragged her back to where they'd left off. White heat radiated from his body into hers, burning away her cobwebs of misgivings. This was nothing like that tainted, ancient memory from years ago. It was sweet and good and right.

Amy felt safe and cherished in these arms that could crush, but didn't. His mouth rocked across hers, seducing and ravaging, giving as much as he took. He stole soft bites of her tingling lips, and the heat in his eyes sent shimmering want through her limbs.

"Will anyone come in?" She wasn't ashamed of what they were doing, but she dreaded another discovery.

"No," he murmured, adding, "But let's make sure."

He moved as if they were dancing, smoothly pivoting her before he caught her hand and swirled her toward an unassuming door. It led to an anteroom and from there they entered a massive bedroom.

This was the king's chamber, a mix of the palace's opulence and Luca's spare, disciplined personality. Huge glass doors led to a terrace that overlooked the sundial and the sea. The glass was covered in sheer drapes that turned the light pale gold. The marble floor was softened with a thick rug in shades of gold and green, the ceiling painted a soothing blue between the white plaster and gold filigree. There was a fireplace and a comfortable sitting area, and a button that he touched caused all the doors to click.

"We have complete privacy now. Even the phone won't ring."

He turned to her and she stepped into his arms with a sigh of gladness, wanting to be swept away again into that place where second thoughts were impossible.

He cupped her face. His spiky lashes flickered as he scanned her features.

"What's wrong?" she asked, uncertainty creeping in.

"Absolutely nothing, but if we only have today, I'm damned well going to take my time and remember every second."

"Oh," she breathed. His words dismantled her at a very basic level. She wasn't that special. Didn't he realize that? She was actually tarnished and broken. What she was doing right now with him was akin to stealing.

But as the pad of his thumb slid across her bottom lip, she whispered, "I want to savor you, too." She lifted a hand to touch his hair, startled to find the strands so soft and fine when it looked so thick.

He adjusted their stance so their bodies aligned perfectly. His feet bracketed hers, and his thighs were hard against her own. He was aroused, the stiffness of him undeniable against the part of her that was growing soft and damp and ripe.

She slid her arms around his strong neck. His touch slipped under her jacket so his hands splayed across her back while they crashed their mouths together.

Something wanton in her wanted—needed—to know he was as helpless against her as she was against him. She arched, inciting him with a grind of her hips against that alluring ridge of hardness, seeking the pressure of him *there*.

Lust exploded between them. His whole body jolted, and his arms tightened before he backed her toward the high bed.

Her thighs and bottom came up against the edge of the mattress. He held her there, pinned against the soft resistance while his legs went between hers. Now he was the one who gave muted thrusts, his gaze holding hers, watching as she released a soft mew of helpless, divine pleasure. She felt herself dissolving.

"Good?"

He had to know it was. She couldn't even speak, only nod and brace her hands on the mattress behind her, arching to encourage his rhythm, sharp heels liable to snag his expensive carpet and who the hell cared because this was the most incredible experience of her life. Every breath was filled with his scent. All of her muscles were shaking with sexual excitement.

His hands swept forward and opened her jacket so he could roam his hot palms over the lime-green camisole she wore. A tickling touch danced across her chest and shoulders as he spread the jacket to expose all of her torso. The hot caress of his hands enclosed her breasts.

She groaned and he caught that with his mouth. His thumbs worked over her nipples through the layers of silk and lace. His tongue brushed against hers, and she groaned again as the coiling pleasure in her center became a molten heat. An unstoppable, screaming force.

She had wanted to push him past his own control and here she was losing hers, fists clenched in his bedspread, hips bucking with greed.

When he lifted his head, she dragged her eyes open, dreading how smug he must be at doing this to her, but she saw only a glow of barely leashed lust in his sharp gaze. He was with her, deep in the eye of the hurricane.

"What do you need?" His voice was a rasp that made her skin tighten. "This?" His head dipped and his mouth was on her breast, fingers pulling aside her camisole and the cup of her bra. His touch snaked across her nipple before he exposed it and enveloped her in the intense heat of his mouth.

A lightning bolt of pleasure went straight to where they were fused at the hips and she groaned, moving helplessly against that lethal shape lodged in the notch of her thighs. Acute sensations were taking over, heat and pleasure and a need so great she couldn't resist succumbing to it.

As he pulled on her nipple, a muted climax rose and broke and cascaded shimmering sensations through her.

Ragged noises left her lips as his hand replaced his mouth, tucking inside the cup of her bra to hold her breast as his mouth came back to hers, tender yet rough, soothing, but determined to catch all of her moans.

The pleasure continued to twist inside her, sweet and delicious and teasingly unsatisfying. She was more aroused than ever. Ready to do *anything*, which caused a twinge of anxiety as she weakly sank onto her back on the mattress, legs still dangling off the side, essentially offering herself to him.

He stayed hovering over her. He could persuade her to do anything right now, she acknowledged. He stood with his thighs between her splayed ones, his thick erection pressed indelibly to the swollen, aching flesh between her legs.

He could have lorded her abandonment over her, especially because she was lifting her hips in a muted plea.

He looked wild, though. Barbaric in the most controlled way possible. If he was an animal, he was the kind that might chase his mate to ground, but he would kill *for* her before he'd allow her to be harmed in any way.

Amy might have reached past that veil of savagery if she'd wanted to, but as he raked his hand down the front of his shirt, tearing the buttons loose and baring his chest, she was lost. He was pushed to the limits of his restraint, and she was bizarrely reassured since she had no ability to resist him, either.

His shirt landed on the floor, and he popped the button on the fly of her new green trousers. His hand swept up, urging her to lift her arms. He lifted her jacket up and threw it off the far side of the mattress. She left her arms up so he could sweep the camisole up and away, as well.

His nostrils flared at the sight of her bare belly

and pale breast overflowing the dislodged cup of her green bra, she arched to tease him with the sight, inviting him to skim his hand behind her back to find the hook.

He whisked away the bra, then traced each shadow and curve of her torso, claiming her with tickling touches and firm flicks of his thumbs. He bent to nuzzle her skin with his lips, pooling his hot breath in the hollow of her collarbone before taking a blatant taste of each pouting nipple, leaving them erect and gleaming.

The zipper of her pants gave with a snap as his hands raked them down her hips.

She didn't protest the damage. She was too caught up in the urgency he was projecting. It was mesmerizing to see the intensity in him as he dragged her pants down her legs and gave each cuff a yank to pull them free of her shoes.

"I can take them off."

"I don't want you to," he said, voice distant, fingertips sliding across the sensitive skin on the top of her feet and encircling her ankles. "I want to do this."

He set the shoes on his shoulders as he lowered to his knees beside the bed.

She strangled her groan of helplessness with the back of her wrist, lost before he'd even touched her.

He delicately moved side the damp silk of her panties. His touch traced between her folds, making her groan again and twist in tortured anticipation.

In the self-conscious knowledge he was looking and touching and—

She gasped as his mouth grazed the inside of her thigh, then the other one. He slowly, slowly kissed toward her center.

She shifted her feet so she could urge him with a heel in his back—forgetting the sharp shoe until he laughed starkly and said, "*That's* what I wanted."

His hot chuckle was her only warning before his mouth was on her and she nearly came off the bed. No restraint in him now. He claimed her unabashedly, tasting, teasing, learning, then mercilessly pleasuring her until she had her thighs locked to his ears.

"Luca. Luca." She lost all inhibition, fist knotted in his hair and hips lifting to meet the swirling pressure of his tongue.

This time her orgasm shattered her. It was one crescendo after another because he made it so, continuing to pleasure her as each wrenching burst of joy contracted through her. He didn't stop until her weak, quivering thighs fell open.

Then he rose to survey the destruction he'd caused. She was in pieces before him, stomach quivering, limbs weak. She was no longer autonomous. She belonged to him.

Which made the way he paused as he hooked his hand in her knickers somewhat laughable, but she lifted her hips in silent consent. Satisfaction came into his stark features then, along with an undisguised possessiveness. His gaze swept down her nudity as he drew the wisp of green off her ankles.

His gaze came back to hers, glints of untamed desire in his fiery blue eyes.

That primeval heat called to her. Drew her to sit up on the edge of the bed and reach a hand to the back of his neck to drag him into kissing her.

His hands went down her bare back and cupped her bottom as he thrust his tongue between her lips, flagrantly making love to her mouth. She sucked on his tongue and blindly fumbled his fly open, then slid her hand inside the elastic of his boxer briefs to clasp the thickness of his shaft and trace her touch to caress his wet tip.

He tangled his hand in her hair and kissed her so deeply, she could hardly breathe, especially when his hand arrived at her breast, reawakening all her erogenous zones as he delicately pinched her nipple.

She squeezed him in reaction, and that seemed to be his snapping point.

He lurched back and shoved his pants down, taking his underwear at the same time. His shoes were toed off and he was naked in seconds, reaching to the nightstand drawer.

She should have removed her own shoes, but she was too caught up in watching his deft movements. He smoothed a condom into place and moved to stand before her.

Her bones softened and she melted onto her back. Intense pleasure was stamped into his expression and his hands went over her, claiming hip and waist and breast and belly and the tender heat between her thighs as he spread her legs to make room for himself. His elbow hooked under one of her knees and he pushed her farther onto the bed so he could get his knee onto the mattress between her own.

His gaze snagged on her shoe where her leg was draped over his arm. "Perhaps I do have a fetish after all."

He lined himself up against her entrance and watched her face as he began to press into her.

She bit her lip.

He paused.

"Don't stop," she gasped. "It just so good."

Her eyes were wet with some emotion between joy and intense need, her sheath slick and welcoming his intrusion with shivering arousal. She couldn't touch enough of him—shoulders, chest, straining neck, the fine strands of his hair on his head.

He made a noise that was a mangled agreement and let his weight ease him deeper, sliding all the way in and coming down onto his elbow so he hovered over her. Her one leg was hooked high on his arm. His free hand tangled in her hair and his mouth covered hers.

She wrapped her arms around his neck and arched her back, signaling how eager she was for the feel of him moving over her. Within her.

He began to thrust.

It was mind-bendingly good. She brought her free

leg up to wrap around his waist and felt his knees bracket her backside. He rocked them and pushed his arm under her lower back, lifting her hips so he could thrust more freely. With more power.

The new angle caused his next thrust to send a hot spear of intense pleasure through her, one that had her tearing her mouth from his to cry out with tormented joy.

His mouth went to her ear and he sucked on her lobe while their heat and energy built. Their love-making turned raw and primal, then. The room filled with their anguished grunts of growing tension and clawing need.

"I need you deeper. Harder," she begged, pulling at his hair.

He caught her other leg and released his full strength, holding back nothing as he drove her higher and higher up the scales of what she could bear.

"Don't stop," she demanded. Pleaded. "Luca! Luca!"

"Let go. You're killing me," he growled, holding both of them trapped on a precipice with his rhythmic, powerful thrusts. "I won't come until you do and I *need* to."

His jagged voice pulled at her while his hard body shifted over her, his mouth taking hers. He surrounded her so fully, there was barely any place he didn't touch. Didn't claim. She was all his. At the mercy of his unconstrained sexual heat.

He slammed into her and rocked against her swollen, delirious flesh. The universe opened into an expansive void. For an infinite moment, they were suspended like stars in the universe, caught in the peak of supreme perfection for all eternity.

Then his tongue touched hers and reality folded in on itself. Orgasm struck like a hammer, and she was moaning against his own noises of supreme gratification while waves of culmination rolled over them, again and again.

Luca woke to the sound of the door locks releasing.

He kept his head buried in his pillow, willing himself to let her go.

"Just once" had turned into twice. Twice was not a slip of control. Twice was unabashed self-indulgence. He had deafened himself to his internal voices of caution and abandoned himself to sheer lust. It had been incredible.

And disturbing to realize he was so capable of immersing himself in base desire. He was not so far above his father as he liked to believe. He was just as capable of pursuing immediate gratification.

When sexual exhaustion had crept over them, he'd thrown himself into a hard nap so he wouldn't have to face this reckoning—which was another facet of abandoned responsibility. On the few occasions when he had made a mistake, Luca always confronted and corrected it. He didn't play denial games.

Sleeping with Amy was definitely a mistake. He'd

known it even as her name had left his lips after their lunch. He should have let her walk away.

At least he was doing it now. She was making it easy for him by slipping away while she thought he was sleeping. He would make it easy for her by not trying to stop her, even though his shoulders twitched with the need to come up on his elbows. *Wait*, hovered unspoken on his lips.

What time was it? Beyond his lowered eyelids and the mound of the pillow, he had the sense that daylight was fading. He didn't look. He held still with belated but ruthless control, waiting to hear the door close behind her.

The sound came from the wrong side of the room. The air moved. It tasted cool and carried the scent of the sea. He lifted his head and glanced toward the terrace.

The sight of her knocked his breath out of him.

Amy, bare-legged and shoeless, strawberry blonde hair streaked with gold wafting loosely down the back of his rippling shirt, was backlit by one of Vallia's signature sunsets.

A trick of air and water currents beyond their west coast caused wispy clouds to gather on the horizon at the end of the day, providing a canvas for dying rays. As the air cooled, the sea calmed to reflect sharp, bright oranges that bled toward streaks of pink and purple while indigo crept in from the edges. Couples came from around the world to photograph their wedding against it.

Luca rose and was outside before he'd consciously thought to join her. He was *drawn*. That power she exerted without effort should have scared the hell out of him, but he was too enchanted by the expression on her face when he came alongside her.

She had moved to the northern end of the terrace and was looking back toward the castle ruins where the colors of the sunset were painting the gray stones bronze and red, throwing its cracks and crevices into dark relief.

He joined her and took in her profile with the same wonder she was sending toward the castle. Her mouth was soft, eyes lit with awe. Her creamy skin held the magical glow off the horizon.

"This is so beautiful. I've never seen anything like it."

"Me, either." The compliment was meant to be ironic, but his voice was lodged in his chest where thick walls were fracturing and tumbling apart.

He gave in to the compulsion to draw her into his arms. His hand found the curve of her bare backside beneath the fall of his shirt, and he reveled in the way his caress fractured her breath.

Let her go, the infernal voice inside him whispered. It was more of a distant howl, like wolves warning of the perils that stalked him if he continued to linger with her.

But she was fragrant and soft and shorter without her heels. She sent him a smoky, womanly smile as she realized he was naked and traced patterns at the base of his spine that tightened his buttocks with pleasure.

Her expression grew somber. Vulnerable. "Thank you for this. I haven't been with anyone in a long time. I needed to know I could be intimate with a man and not lose everything."

Tension invaded his limbs. Not jealousy or possessiveness, but a primitive protectiveness that tasted similar. His arms unconsciously tightened, wanting to hold on to her because he understood from her remark that she was afraid of being caged again.

She was reminding him this couldn't be anything more than this one day.

He knew it as well as she did, but he moved his hand into her hair and gently dragged her head back, mostly to see if she'd allow it. They'd grown damned familiar in the last couple of hours, and he wanted that small show of trust from her.

Her lips parted in shock while lust hazed her gaze.

A self-deprecating smile tugged at the corners of his mouth. "I should hate myself for enjoying this as much as I do." Her capitulation. The surge of virility it gave him that she allowed him to dominate her this way. He was an animal, just the same as everyone else. He had never wanted to admit that. "Sex was *his* thing. It's hard for me to give in to desire without thinking there's something wrong with me when I do." He had never told that to anyone. He'd barely articulated it to himself. "It's probably best that today is all we have." Otherwise, they might destroy one another.

With absolute gravity, she said, "There is nothing wrong with the way you make love."

They should be exchanging playful banter, preparing for a lighthearted parting. Instead, he kissed her, hard. He wanted to imprint himself on her.

The wolves were continuing to howl, but he let himself absorb the fullness of the moment. The way her nails dug into his scalp as she pressed him to kiss her more deeply, the way her tongue greeted his own... This was all they had. This moment. This kiss.

That's all it should have been. But as the fine hair on her mound tantalized his erection and her toes caressed the top of his foot, his heart pounded hard enough to crack his sternum. "Once more?" he asked through his teeth.

She was as powerless to this force as he was and didn't bother trying to hide it. "Once more," she breathed.

With a savage smile, he pressed her toward the doors. "Get back in my bed then."

Amy woke in the early morning, naked and alone in her bed in the guest suite. She stretched and let out a sigh that was both enjoyment of the luxurious thread count and a half moan as her sore muscles twinged. She was glowing with the lingering sensuality of their lovemaking, but beneath it was despondency.

Once had not been enough, even when it turned into an afternoon and evening.

Yesterday was all they would have, though. One golden memory. She worked for Luca. She had an assignment to complete, one she had neglected because they'd been so wrapped up in each other. She'd stolen from his room near midnight like Cinderella, shoes in hand, jacket held in front of her to hide her broken fly. A footman had escorted her, but she trusted he wouldn't say a word.

She was starving and desperate for coffee, so she rose to find the French press in the kitchen. There was cheese, fresh berries and yogurt in the refrigerator, too. Perfect.

She set them out and started the kettle, then went in search of her phone. It was still in her jacket pocket from last night, still set on Do Not Disturb from when she'd joined Luca for lunch. They'd skipped dinner, which was why she was ready to gnaw her own arm.

Still yawning, she touched her thumb to unlock her phone and it flashed to life with notifications. She had several alerts set for her own name since she was often attached to press releases for clients, but this wasn't a press release.

It was about her client. And *her*.

The photos showed her and Luca with the sunset behind them, and each headline slanted them into a different, damning light.

Like Father, Like Son! one headline blared.

The king of Vallia continues a tradition of depravity by seducing his new hire, socialite Amy
Miller of London Connection, who caused a
stir in the late queen's foundation with her publicity campaign for an upcoming gala…

Victim or Villain? the next asked while the photo's angle revealed her seductive profile and Luca's
riveted expression.

The Golden Prince is dragged into the gutter
by a gold digger…

Crown Jewels on Display! screamed the most taw-
dry headline.

They'd blurred the photo, but she knew he'd been
naked and fully aroused.

"Oh, Luca," she whispered.

How had something so perfect and unsullied become…this?

As her unblinking eyes grew hot, Amy sank onto
the sofa, crushed by the magnitude of this develop-
ment. Her stomach churned while her brain exploded
with the infinite agonies that were about to befall
her—the sticks and stones and betrayals and blame.

Her life would disintegrate. Again.

And, just like last time, she had no one to blame
but herself.

CHAPTER SEVEN

"Photos were published overnight, *signor*. They are...unfortunate."

"Of *who*?" It was a testament to how thoroughly Amy had numbed his brain that he didn't compute immediately that it was, of course, about the two of them.

Guillermo thrust a tablet under his nose.

Luca's head nearly exploded. The foulest language he'd ever uttered came out of his throat. "Where the *hell* was security?"

"They went up to the castle as soon as they realized they had a stray hiker, but he had already departed."

The guards wouldn't have sensed any urgency. Despite the regulations against visiting the ruins without a guide, the odd tourist still made their way up there, usually photographing the silhouette of the palace against the sunset. Since the lighting was so poor at that time of day, and all the private rooms faced the sea, the chance of compromising a royal family member was low. The paparazzi who'd made the trek had never struck pay dirt because even Luca's father hadn't been stupid enough to stand naked on the *one* visible corner of the terrace.

"We presume it was taken by an amateur," Guillermo continued stiffly. "Given the photo's quality and the fact it was initially posted to a private account. The images have since been reposted by the tabloids with... As you can see."

Unspeakable headlines.

Golden Prince: Feet of Clay, Rod of Steel?

At least they'd blurred his erection, but they'd set his image beside a grainy one of his father in a miniscule swimsuit.

King of Vallia Inherits the Horny Crown

When he saw *Another Molesting Monarch*, he thought he might throw up.

"The PR team is discussing damage control. I've made arrangements for Ms. Miller to return to London."

Luca barely heard him. For his entire life, he had kept to the straight and narrow and the *one time* he had stepped out of line, he was caught and being compared to his father in the most abhorrent way—

Wait. His heart clunked its gears, shifting from

reflexive shame and fury to a glimmer of possibility. This was bad. But was it bad *enough*?

This wasn't the scandal he'd wanted. Amy was being derided as badly as he was, but his heart lurched into a gallop as he suddenly spotted the finish line after a marathon that had gone on for two decades.

"She'll be mobbed in London," Luca said, his mind racing. "She doesn't go anywhere until I've spoken to her. PR doesn't take steps without my input."

Guillermo's mouth tightened, but he moved to the door to relay that instruction.

Luca drummed his fingers on his desk. This was far messier and more degrading than he'd wanted it to be, but he would owe London Connection an efficiency bonus if it worked.

It had to work. He would *make* it work.

"Has my sister been informed?"

"A secure line has been established." Guillermo nodded at the landline on Luca's desk. "The Privy Council is divided on how to react." He looked like he'd swallowed a fish hook. "Some are alarmed and suggesting a review of the line of succession. I did try to warn you, *signor.* I *strongly* suggest Ms. Miller be returned to London—"

"I'll speak to my sister." With a jerk of his head, Luca dismissed him.

"I can't believe you did that," Sofia said. There was no ring of outrage or remnants of the second-hand embarrassment they'd both suffered after their father's various exploits. No, there was a far deeper note of stunned comprehension in her tone.

Luca bit back trying to explain it wasn't how he'd meant for this to happen. It was worse and he was genuinely embarrassed, but this was their chance. They had to run with it.

Also, focusing on his goal allowed him to side-step dealing with the fact he was now the poster boy of depravity.

"You have no choice but to take this to the nanny panel," he said gravely, using their childhood reference to the ring of advisers, now the Privy Council, which kept such a tight leash on both of them. The same ones who had insisted Luca take the throne despite Sofia being entitled to it by birth.

"My travel is already being arranged. I'll meet with them the minute I'm home. I've drafted a statement that I'll release the minute we hang up." She paused, then asked with soft urgency, "Are you *sure*, Luca? Because I'm taking a very assertive stance on this. I don't want to undermine you."

"Sofia. Be the ruler you *are*. It's what is best for Vallia. Don't worry about me."

"Impossible. You're my one and only brother." She took a steadying breath. He thought she might be choking up with emotion, but she was well practiced in keeping a cool head. She cleared her throat. Her voice was level as she continued. "I have questions that can wait, but I plan to make the case for you to stay on as my heir provided you're willing to express your sincere regret and assurance that nothing like this will ever happen again?"

Which part? Being caught naked with a woman? Trysting with an employee? Or making love to Amy in particular?

Some nascent emotion, a grasping sense of opportunity, rose in him, but he firmly quashed it before it could become a clear desire. An *intention*.

Their "just once" might have turned into three times, but their connection was exposed to the entire world, and it was completely inappropriate. *He* didn't want to be labeled the sort of man who took advantage of women in his employ.

"You have my word," he said, feeling a tear inside him as he made the vow.

"*Grazie.* I'll see you soon. *Ti amo*," Sofia said.

"I love you, too." Luca hung up and a cool chill washed over him, like damp air exhaled from a dark cave. It was done.

Amy hadn't stopped shaking, even after a hot shower and too many cups of scalding coffee. The fact that she couldn't seem to leave this room, let alone this palace or this country, didn't help at all.

"I'll pay for the taxi myself," she beseeched the maid, Fabiana.

"It's not my place to call one, *signorina*." Fabiana set out ravioli tossed with gleaming cherry tomatoes and pesto. It looked as scrumptious as the fluffy omelet Amy had ignored midmorning, the focaccia she'd snubbed at lunch and the afternoon tea of crustless sandwiches and pastries she'd disregarded a few hours ago.

There was only room in her stomach for nausea. Her whole world was imploding, and she couldn't even reach out to the best friends who had got her through a similar crisis in the past. Her Wi-Fi connection had been cut off while she'd still been reeling in shock.

Then an ultra-calm middle-aged woman had appeared and identified herself as the senior Human Resources manager for the palace. She was genuinely concerned and had urged Amy to "be honest" if her night with Luca had been coerced in any way.

Amy had insisted it was consensual, but she now wondered if she'd strengthened Luca's position and hindered her own.

She was cold all over, sickened that she'd let this happen and angry with herself because she knew better. She had been fully aware of the potential dangers in sleeping with him, and she had gone ahead and put herself in this awful position anyway.

"My instructions are to ensure you're as comfortable as possible," Fabiana was saying. "Is there anything else I can bring you?"

"Hiking boots," Amy muttered peevishly. She had already asked a million times to speak to Luca. She'd been assured he would see her as soon as he was available.

Fabiana dropped her gaze to the bedroom slippers Amy was wearing with yellow pajama pants and a silk T-shirt. "I wouldn't recommend trying to leave on foot. Paparazzi are stalking the perimeter. Security is very tight at the moment."

Amy hugged the raw silk shawl she'd found in the closet and wrapped around her shoulders. "Restore my Wi-Fi." It wasn't the first time she'd asked for that, either.

"I've passed along your request. I'll mention it again." Fabiana gave her yet another pained smile and hurried out.

Amy was so frustrated, she stomped out the doors of her lounge to the garden patio.

A security guard materialized from the shrubbery. He'd been there all day and once again held up a staying hand. "I'm sorry—"

She whirled back inside.

She needed to get back to London. She needed to know exactly how bad this was. How could she control the damage to London Connection if she was cut off like this?

She ached to talk to Bea and Clare. What must they be thinking of her? She'd told them she was dropping everything for a big fish client with a substantial budget and an "unusual request." Would they question her tactics in getting Luca's business? They had stood by her last time, but they would be fully entitled to skepticism of her motives, especially since her actions were jeopardizing their livelihood along with her own.

Amy's mother was likely having fits, too. Even without a call or text, Amy knew what Deborah Miller was thinking. *Again, Amy? Again?*

She felt so helpless! Crisis management was her bread and butter. She ought to be able to *do* something. As she paced off her tension, she took some comfort in methodically thinking through her response.

In any emergency, there were three potential threats to consider. The first was physical safety. This wasn't a chemical spill. Innocent bystanders weren't being harmed. She forced herself to release a cleansing breath and absorb that tiny blessing.

The second threat was financial loss. She sobered as she accepted that she would take a hard hit from this. There was no way she was taking Luca's money now. That meant all of the expenses for this trip along with the travel home were hers. She had reassigned several of her contracts to other agents at London Connection so she had lost a substantial amount of income. There would be costs to salvaging London Connection's reputation and, since this was her mistake, she would bear that, as well.

How would she pay for it all?

Here was where panic edged in each time she went through this exercise. She was standing hip deep in the third type of threat. Her credibility was in tatters.

She looked like a woman who slept her way into contracts and had no means to spin that impression. In fact, somewhere in this palace, a team of professionals exactly like her was deciding how to rescue Luca from this crisis, and Amy knew exactly the approaches they were taking—deflect the attacks on him. Blame her. Claim she had seduced him. Say she had set him up for that photo to raise the profile of London Connection.

Heck, the headlines she'd glimpsed before losing her connection had already been suggesting she'd had something to gain. They only had to build on what was already there.

What if they found out she had a history of inappropriate relationships?

Her stomach wrenched so violently, she folded her arms across it, moaning and nearly doubling over.

Luca wouldn't hang her out to dry like that. Would he?

Of course, he would. The teacher, Avery Mason, had. The headmistress and her own parents had.

In a fit of near hysteria, she barged out of her suite to the hall.

She surprised the guard so badly, he took on a posture of attack, making her stumble back into her doorway, heart pounding.

She was so light-headed, she had to cling to the doorjamb. She sounded like a harridan when she blurted, "Tell the king I'll set my room on fire if he doesn't speak to me in the next ten minutes. Punch me unconscious or call the fire brigade because I *will* do it."

The guard caught the door before she could slam it in his face. He spoke Italian into his wrist. After the briefest of pauses, he nodded. "Come with me."

Now she'd done it. He was taking her to a padded cell. Or the dungeon.

Yes, that kind of dungeon.

She sniffed back a semihysterical laugh-sob.

He escorted her through halls that were familiar. She was being taken to Luca's office. The scene of their first criminal kiss. And their second.

People filed out as she arrived, but she didn't make eye contact. She stared at the floor until she was told to go in. She went only as far as she had to for the door to close behind her.

"Will you introduce us, Luca?" a woman asked.

Amy snapped her head up to see only Luca and his sister were in the room.

Luca was as crisp and urbane as ever in a smart suit and tie, freshly shaved with only a hint of fatigue around his eyes to suggest he'd had a long day. His gaze sharpened on her, but Amy was distracted by his twin.

Sofia Albizzi was a feminine version of Luca, almost as tall, also athletically lean, but with willowy curves and a softer expression. Where the energy that radiated off Luca was dynamic and energizing, Sofia's was equally commanding but with a settle-down-children quality. She wore a pantsuit in a similar dark blue as Luca's suit. Her hair was in a chignon, and she offered a calm, welcoming smile.

Amy must look like a petitioning peasant, slouched in her shawl and slippers, hair falling out of its clip and no makeup to hide her distress. She felt *awful* coming up against this double barrel of effortless perfection. She wanted to turn and walk back out again, but Luca straightened off the edge of his desk.

"Your Highness, this is Amy Miller. Amy, my sister Sofia, the queen of Vallia."

"Queen?" Amy distantly wondered if she was supposed to curtsy.

Sofia flicked a glance at Luca that could only be described as sibling telepathy.

"My new title is confidential," Sofia said. "Only finalized within the last hour. There will be a press release in the morning. I hope I can trust you to keep this information to yourself until then?"

Amy choked on disbelief. "Who could I tell? You've cut off my online access."

"We did do that," Sofia acknowledged. "The prince said you understand the importance of limiting communication during a crisis, so we can project a clear and unified message."

Prince. He'd been dethroned. *By her.* She was definitely going to faint. Amy blinked rapidly, trying to keep her vision from fading as she looked between the two.

Sofia came toward her, regal and ridiculously attractive while exuding that consoling energy. "I appreciate how distressed you must be, Amy. It's been a trying day for all of us, but I hope you'll allow us to show you the best of our hospitality for a little longer? And not frighten staff with threats of setting the palace on fire?"

Emotion gathered in Amy's eyes, beleaguered humor and frustration and something that closed her throat because she suddenly had the horrid feeling she had disappointed Sofia. Not the way she consistently disappointed her mother. She wasn't being held to impossible, superficial standards. No, Sofia simply projected a confidence that Amy was better than someone who made wild threats. *Let's all do better*, she seemed to say.

Luca was right. She was an ideal ruler.

But there was no comfort in being the instrument that had installed her on the throne, not when it had cost her the life she'd worked so hard to build.

"I want to go h-home." She was at the end of her thin, frayed rope.

"Our people will arrange that soon," Sofia began, but Luca came forward with purpose.

"I'll walk you to your room."

Sofia shot him a look, but Luca avoided her questioning gaze and held the door for Amy.

From the moment the photos had emerged, he had been buried in meetings, phone calls and demands for his attention. He felt as though he'd gone twelve rounds, taking hits from every angle.

It was *not* in his nature to throw a fight. Keeping his mouth shut while his sister called for an HR investigation had been particularly humiliating. To protect the integrity of that report, he hadn't spoken to Amy.

While they'd awaited a determination on whether Amy had been harassed by Luca, other factions had proposed throwing her to the wolves of public opinion to save Luca's reputation. Several voices on the council had tried to cast him as the victim of a scheming woman, eager to make excuses for Luca's lapse in judgment so they could maintain the status quo.

Sofia's supporters had been equally quick to question what kind of queen Amy would make, forcing Luca to declare his intentions toward her.

"We seized a moment, that's all." He hated to reduce her to a one-night stand, but it was what they had agreed and it was better for her to be seen as collateral damage, not a contributor.

"The media storm will rage forever unless we take decisive action," Sofia had pressed. "No matter how we attempt to explain it away, the photos will be reposted every time the king of Vallia is mentioned."

"I've become synonymous with our father," Luca said grimly, hating that it was true, hating that this was the only way, but he threw himself on the proverbial sword. "I won't have his transgressions pinned on me." On that he wouldn't budge. "Vallia's queens have always been bastions of dignity and honor. If I step aside, that's what you'll have again."

That had been the turning point. Discussions had moved from if to how.

Luca had spared a thought to ensure Amy's comfort, but he hadn't allowed memories of last night to creep in. It would have destroyed his concentration.

That fog of desire was making him light-headed now, but he continued to fight it. He had sworn his misstep wouldn't be repeated. His libido might have other desires, but tomorrow his sister would take the crown and Luca would once again become the Golden Prince, honorable to a fault.

Nevertheless, he owed Amy an explanation for how things had played out today.

"It's standard protocol to shut down all the open networks and allow only secure messaging when incidents occur," he told her as they walked. "And I wanted to shield you from the worst of what's happening online."

"I understand." She nodded jerkily, looking like a ghost.

A pocket of gravel formed in the pit of his gut, a heaviness of conscience he wasn't familiar with because he so rarely made mistakes.

"I assumed you would have an idea what was going on behind the scenes."

"I did." She was nothing but eyes and cheekbones and white lips, her profile shell-shocked.

It hit him that she did know—all too well. He wanted to stop and touch her. Draw her into his arms. Kiss her and swear he wasn't pinning the blame on her.

He settled for following her into her suite.

"I couldn't bring you into the discussions today. I realize, given our contract, that you expected to be consulted, but I had to sideline you. It was best to let the process play out through normal channels."

"You think I'm upset because I feel 'sidelined'? I wish I was a footnote! Why didn't you tell me we were exposed out there? Did you *plan* this?"

"Of course not!" He hadn't given thought to anything but *her* last night. Did she think he would walk outside naked for anyone else? He was still uncomfortable with how immersed he'd been in their mutual desire. "It was a fluke. For God's sake, Amy. How could I plan it?"

"A fluke?" she scoffed. "You just happened to pick *me* to come here and take on the task of *ruining* you. You just happened to kiss me and take me to your room—" She cut herself off, shielding her eyes in what could only be described as shame.

The rocks in his belly began to churn.

"When I heard the door, I thought you were leaving." He started forward, drawn by her distress. "I didn't know you were going outside. I didn't *take* you out there."

As soon as his feet came into her line of sight, she brought up her head and stumbled back, keeping a distance between them.

That retreat, coupled with the trepidation in her face, was like a knee to the groin.

He held very still, holding off a pain that he barely

understood. It was new, but so acute he actually tasted bile in the back of his throat.

"I'm not going to touch you if you don't want me to." He opened his hands in a gesture of peace.

"I don't want you to scramble my head again," she muttered, arms crossed and brow flexing with anguish. "This wasn't supposed to happen, Luca. No one was supposed to know about us. You made me think that's what you wanted."

"It was." But affirming it made his mouth burn. "Look, I know this wasn't the way we planned it, but once the photographs were out there, I had to seize the opportunity. This is what I hired you to do."

"You did *not* hire me to sleep with you. I won't take money for it," she said jaggedly.

He was insulted by her implication. "I hired you to ruin me. You have."

She gasped if he'd struck her. Her hurt and distress were so clear, his arms twitched again to reach for her.

"I honestly thought you would understand this was the incident I needed," he said. "I'm not clear why you're so upset."

"I was supposed to find someone who *wanted* the attention. Someone prepared for it." She kept pulling at her shawl until it was so tight around her, the points of her shoulders and elbows looked as though they would poke holes in the raw silk. "I was supposed to control the message to minimize the damage. It wasn't going to be ugly exposure where a woman's reputation is torn to shreds."

When her gaze flashed to his, there was such agony in the green depths, his heart stalled.

"My team won't crucify you," he swore, and started to take a step forward, but checked himself. "I won't allow it. I'm taking responsibility. This was my slipup—"

"I slept with a client, Luca!" Her arm flung out and the shawl fell off her shoulder. "I compromised him so badly I caused a *king* to be *dethroned*. It really doesn't matter what you or your team say. People will come to their own conclusions."

He briefly glimpsed her tattoo before she shrugged the shawl back into place.

She was shaking so hard, he started to reach for her again and she stumbled back another step.

"I won't touch you." He couldn't help that his voice was clipped with impatience. "But I'm worried about you. Sit down. Have you eaten? I told them to make sure you had food."

"I'm not a dog!" she cried, eyes wild. "You don't get to hire someone to check if I have food and water and call it good. Although, at least I would have got a proper walk today instead of being held like a prisoner."

"That—" He squeezed the back of his neck. "I realize you're angry, but stop saying such ridiculous things."

"Oh! Am I overreacting?" She shot him a look

that threatened to tear his head from his shoulders. "You know nothing about what I'm going through. *Nothing*."

"So explain it to me," he snapped back. "Because I don't see this as the disaster that you do. You said it yourself. People love to clutch their pearls over a sexy escapade. I'm the one who's naked in that photo, not you! Are you upset that *we happened*?" It took everything in him to ask that. It wasn't an accusation, he really needed to know, but he braced himself. "Are you feeling as if I took advantage of you? Like you couldn't say no last night?"

HR had interviewed her. She'd reported that Amy had confirmed their involvement was consensual. Even so, Amy's chin crinkled. Her eyes welled.

His heart lurched and he couldn't breathe.

"I should have said no." Her shoulders sagged. "I knew it was a mistake and I want to take it back." She buried her face in her hands. "So badly."

That sent a streak of injury through him because the thing that unnerved him most was how little he *didn't* regret sleeping with her.

As the dominoes had fallen today, he'd disliked himself for playing manipulative palace politics the way his father had. He'd met the disillusioned gazes of mentors and advisers and understood he'd fallen miles in their estimation. He loathed feeling fallible.

He had suffered through all of that to correct a thirty-one-year-old wrong and, unpleasant as proceedings had all been, at least he had the extraordinary memory of *her* to offset it.

Even now, as he saw how devastated she was over their exposure, he couldn't make himself say he was sorry. Did she remember how much pleasure they'd given each other?

He pushed his hands into his pockets so he wouldn't try to remind her.

"The announcements will be made tomorrow. I'll step down, and Sofia will be recognized as the rightful ruler. My coronation ceremony was scheduled to happen before our parliament sits in the autumn. It will be revised for her, but she's taking control immediately. Let the dust settle on some of this before you assume you'll take the fall for it."

She snorted, despondent, and turned her back on him. She looked like a tree that had been stripped bare. She was a hollow trunk swaying in the dying winds of a storm.

Was she hiding tears?

His guts fell into his shoes and his heart was upside down in his chest. He wanted to take her in his arms, hold her and warm her and swear this would be okay. *Come to my room.* He kept the words in his throat, but they formed a knot that locked up his lungs so his whole torso ached.

"When can I go back online? Bea and Clare are probably frantic." Her voice was a broken husk.

"My people have provided them with a statement."

That had her whirling around to face him, eyes shooting fires of disbelief that were quickly soaked by her welling tears. "You don't speak for me, Luca. You don't get to tell your side without giving me a chance to tell mine!"

"It's only a standard 'not enough information to comment—'"

No use. She disappeared into the bedroom and slammed the door on him.

CHAPTER EIGHT

AMY TOSSED AND TURNED and finally quit fighting her tears. When she let go, she cried until her eyes were swollen and scratchy, then rose and set a cool, wet cloth over them. Her stomach panged so hard with hunger, she dug up cold leftovers the maid had left in the fridge.

It was almost two in the morning. She didn't know if the guard was still in the garden and didn't check. Her one brief thought about trying to run away was stymied by exhaustion.

She crawled back into bed and didn't wake until midmorning when her phone came alive with alerts and notifications. Her internet access had been restored.

Tempted as she was to post *I'm being held against my will*, she was quickly caught up in reading all the news updates, emails and texts along with listening to her voice mail.

She brought her knees up to her chest, cringing as her mother's message began with an appalled "For God's sake, Amy."

Beyond the bedroom door, she heard the maid enter the suite, but kept listening to her mother harangue her for making international headlines "behaving like a trollop."

It wasn't the maid. Her heart lurched as Luca walked into the bedroom with a tray. He was creaseless and stern, emanating the scent of a fresh shower and shave.

Amy was nestled in the pillows she'd piled against the headboard, blankets gathered around her. She clicked off her phone mid maternal diatribe and dropped the device.

"You really have been demoted, haven't you?"

He stilled as he absorbed the remark, then gave her a nod of appreciation. "Nice to have you back. I was worried. Especially when I was told you didn't eat a single bite yesterday. That changes now." He touched something on the tray and legs came down with a snick.

"Your spies don't know what I do when no one is around." She was dying for coffee, though, so she straightened her legs, allowing him to set the tray across her lap.

"They're spies, Amy. Of course, they do." He sat down next to her knees and poured coffee from the carafe into the two cups on the tray.

"Are you really having me watched?" She scowled toward the ceiling corners in search of hidden cameras.

"No." His mouth twitched. "But I'd be lying if I

didn't admit to concern over how you might be handling the restoration of your internet connection. You were very angry last night." He sipped his coffee. "Anything we should know about?"

She followed his gaze to her phone, facedown and turned to silent, but vibrating with incoming messages.

"I've been reading, not responding. My social feeds are on fire. In times like this, you find out very quickly who your real friends are." A handful of clients were ready to die on a hill defending her. Others were asking about terminating their contracts. "Bea and Clare have asked me to call when I can. They won't judge, but I don't know what to tell them. The rest of the office is used to being left in the dark with certain clients or actions we take on their behalf. They're reaching out with thoughts and prayers, but I can tell they're dying of curiosity, wondering if this is a stunt or if I'm really this stupid." Her hand shook as she dolloped cream into her coffee. "Our competitors are reveling in my hypocrisy, of course, crossing professional lines when I'm usually defending victims of such things. They'll dine on this forever, using it to tarnish London Connection's integrity and my competence."

"London Connection won't be impacted." Luca's expression darkened. "I've set up the transfer. That will keep things afloat until you're able to right the ship."

"I told you not to pay me." She clattered her cup

back into the saucer, spilling more coffee than she'd tasted. "I won't accept it. Taking money for this makes me feel cheap and dirty and stupid. Don't make me refuse it again, Luca."

He set his own cup down with a firm clink while he spat out a string of curses and rose to pace restlessly. "You did what I hired you to do," he reminded Amy as he rounded on her. "I want to compensate you."

"I ruined *myself*. I ruined my friends' livelihood."

"Quit being so hard on yourself."

"Quit being so obtuse! Just because I don't run a country doesn't mean my actions don't have consequences." She snatched up her phone and tapped to play her mother's message from the beginning, increasing the volume so Luca got the full benefit of her mother's appalled disgust.

"For God's sake, Amy. You've really done it this time, behaving like the worst sort of trollop. Neville is putting me on a plane back to London. He doesn't want to be associated with me. I've had your father on the phone, too. How can I tell him you're reliable enough to take control of your trust when you do things like this? You really never learn, do you?"

Amy clicked it off so they didn't have to hear the rest.

"I thought you were already disinherited."

"My father has control of a trust fund that was set up for me when I was born. I was supposed to start receiving income from it ten years ago, but I was expelled from school." She didn't tell him why. "They decided I wasn't responsible enough. I was supposed to assume full control at twenty-five, but my career promoting high-society parties online wasn't deemed serious enough. Daddy moved the date to my thirtieth birthday, eighteen months from now. Apparently, that's now off, as well." She threw her phone back into the blankets.

Luca swore again, this time with less heat, more remorse.

"I don't care." It was mostly true. "I've learned to live without their financial support. But when I took your contract, I had a fantasy of finally telling them to shove it. I wanted to prove I'd made my fortune my own way, which was pure pride on my part. Looks like I've got more time to make that dream come true. Problem solved," she said with facetious cheer while bitterness and failure swirled through her chest.

Why was life such a game of chutes and ladders? Why did she always hit the long slide back to zero?

"I had no idea." He came back to sit on the bed.

"Why would you?" She wrapped her cold hands around the hot cup of coffee, ignoring that it was wet down one side. She couldn't help fearing her earlier mistake with Avery Mason would emerge. It had been covered up, and all the key players had more reason to hide it than expose it, but it was still there, lurking like a venomous snake in the grass.

His firm hand gripped her calf through the blankets. "You have to let me help you, Amy."

"Luca." She jerked her leg away. "If you offer me that money one more time, you're going to get a cup of hot coffee in the face. It will turn into a whole thing with your bodyguards, and I'll wind up Tasered and rotting in jail. Not the best path to saving my reputation so leave it alone."

He didn't back off one iota. He found her leg again and gave it a squeeze. "Are you really prone to arson and violence?"

"No," she admitted dourly. "But after my own parents left me fending for myself at eighteen, I've become hideously independent. The worst thing you could have done yesterday was leave me alone like this, helpless to solve my problem."

"Because it's not your problem," he insisted. "That's why I didn't ask you to solve it." He shifted so he was looking at the wall, elbows on his knees, hands linked between them. He sighed. "I didn't see how much damage this would do to you. I want to help you fix it, Amy. Tell me what I can do."

She sank heavily into the pillows. "If I had a clue how to fix it, I would have busted out of here and done it already."

"Let me talk to your parents. I'll take responsibility, patch things up."

"Pass. There's too much water under the bridge there…" Her nose stung with old tears she refused to shed. "And I don't want someone to talk them into forgiving me. I want them to want to help me because they love me." She was embarrassed that they didn't and turned her mind from dwelling on that old anguish since it would never be resolved. "I'm more worried about London Connection. I might have to resign."

"You're not losing your career because you did your job," he said forcefully.

"No one can know that, though, can they? To the outside world, I got involved with a client and caused him to lose *his* job. No one is going to hire the sordid one-night stand who caused a king to be overthrown. If I resign, London Connection can at least say they cleaned house in the same way that Vallia is dumping you."

"That's rubbish." He rose again, all his virile energy crackling around him like a halo. "You're not a martyr and you're not a tramp. You're not something that needs to be swept under a rug or out a door. The answer is obvious."

"A tell-all to the highest bidder?" she suggested with a bat of her lashes.

"Pass," he said with flat irony. "No. Once Sofia is clearly established as Vallia's queen, you and I will take control of our narrative, as you like to say. We'll reframe our affair as a more serious relationship."

"You want to keep sleeping together?" Shock echoed within her strained words.

He wanted that so badly, he had to stand on the far side of the room so he wouldn't crowd her or otherwise pressure her into it. "Appear to, at least. I understand if you'd prefer to keep things professional."

"Because we're so good at *that*." Her chuckle was semihysterical.

He took perverse comfort from the helplessness in her choked laugh. He wasn't the only one who felt this irresistible pull between them.

"I'm just saying, now that I fully grasp how our affair complicates things for you—"

The noise she made drew his glance.

"Do I *not* understand?" He narrowed his eyes, noting the flush that had come into her cheeks, the glow of disgrace in her eyes. "Is there more?"

She bit the corner of her mouth and dropped her gaze. "There are things in my past I only share on a need-to-know basis. Right now, you don't need to know."

She set aside the tray and flung back the blankets. She wore a silk nightgown that rode up her bare legs as she slid her feet to the floor.

"Don't you have a throne to abdicate?" she asked.

He swallowed and forced his gaze upward to the suppressed turmoil in hers.

She was trying to throw him off with a glimpse of her legs and her air of nonchalance.

He couldn't pretend he wasn't falling for the diversion. Sexual awareness instantly throbbed like a drumbeat between them. His feet ambled him closer before he remembered he was trying to give her space.

"I do have a title to renounce," he confirmed, gaze drawn to the way oyster-colored lace coyly pretended to hide her cleavage. It took everything in him to only caress her pale skin with his eyes. "Then I have a gala to attend. *We* do."

"I'm not convinced our continuing to see one another is the best way forward." Her head shake was more of an all-over tremble.

He closed his fists so he wouldn't reach for her. "If you go scurrying home in disgrace, you really will be painted as the scarlet woman who toppled a kingdom. If you stick around and attend the gala where the new queen will speak to you, the whole thing will be reduced to a family squabble between my sister and I. You made arrangements to be here for two weeks, didn't you?"

"Yes, but—"

"You don't have to decide this instant. Let me finish my business, then we'll talk more. Away from the palace," he said. "We'll shop for a gown for the gala. Do you prefer Paris or Milan for evening wear?"

"The Glam Shed," she said haughtily, giving her hair a flick. "I quid pro quo promotion campaigns for red carpet rentals."

"I'll pretend that was a joke and make arrangements for Milan. It's closer than Paris and I have a cottage in Northern Italy. We can talk there about how we'll portray our relationship." For the first time in a very long time, he could be with a woman openly with few distractions. He wanted to take her there right now.

Perhaps she read that urgency in him. She flashed him a nervous look, but there was no fright in the depths of her pretty green eyes. Only a vacillating nibble of her lip and another, slower study of his chest and upper arms.

She was going to be the death of him, teasing him so unconsciously and effortlessly.

"Cottage?" she asked skeptically.

He tilted his head. It was an understatement. "A castle on a private island in one of the more remote lakes. The key word is 'private.' We can let this furor die down before our attendance at the gala stirs it up again."

"Are you sure you want to continue associating with me?" she asked anxiously.

She couldn't be that obtuse.

"I want to do a damned sight more than 'associate.'" He snagged her hand with his own and brought her fingertips to his mouth, dying to taste her from brows to ankles, but he had places to be. And he was trying not to take when she was vacillating and vulnerable.

She caught her breath and looked at him with such defenseless yearning, he gave in and swooped his free hand behind her waist to draw her close.

She suddenly balked with a press of her palm to his chest. "I haven't brushed my teeth."

"Then I'll kiss you here." He set his open mouth

against her throat, enjoying the gasp she released and the all-over shiver that chased down her body. By the time he'd found the hollow beneath her ear, she was melting into him with another soft cry.

The slippery silk she wore was warm with the heat of her body as he slid his hands to her lower back and drew her closer, inhaling the scent of vanilla and almonds from her hair.

"Luca." She nuzzled his ear and nipped at his earlobe.

His scalp tightened and a sharp pull in his groin threatened to empty his head of everything except the rumpled bed behind this wickedly tempting woman. One quick tumble to hold him. That's all he wanted.

"Give me a few hours," he groaned, lifting his head, but running his touch to her delectable bottom, tracing the curve and crease through the silk as he drew her into the stiffness her response had provoked. "We'll pick this up later."

She searched his gaze, still conflicted.

He kissed her, quickly and thoroughly, tasting coffee as he grazed her tongue with his.

"Eat something," he ordered, then released her and adjusted himself before he left to end his brief reign.

Amy ate. Then she took her time with a long bath and a quiet hour of self-care where she painted her toenails and plucked her brows and moisturized every inch of her skin. She ignored her phone and let the sickening feeling of having her privacy invaded recede while she considered what to tell her best friends.

She was always honest with Bea and Clare, but aside from emailing a promise to call as soon as she could, Amy hadn't found the right way to explain what had happened between her and Luca.

They would know they were being put off, but Amy would touch base with them as soon as she decided whether she would agree to Luca's suggestion.

He had a point that appearing to continue their affair would soften the photo from being a lurid glimpse at a king's downfall to a private moment between a loving couple, but they weren't a loving couple. They were barely a romantic couple, having met only two days ago.

It shocked her to realize that. They'd shared some very personal details with one another. She'd never talked about her expulsion or her parents' rejection of her so candidly. For his part, Luca had entrusted her with the secret of his father's death. On a physical level, they had opened themselves unreservedly.

That meant they had the seeds of a close relationship, didn't it?

Oh, Amy, she chided herself. She had made the mistake of believing physical infatuation meant genuine caring once before.

Her stomach curdled. She hadn't shared *that* part of her story with Luca, had she?

Her affair with Avery Mason wouldn't come out, would it? Aside from Bea and Clare, who would never betray her, the story had never been confirmed. If any of the catty girls from back then had wanted to take Amy down by repeating that morsel of vague gossip, they would have done it by now. They'd had plenty of opportunities while Amy had been posting photos of herself with movie stars and fashion designers. Even if someone did decide to bring it up, they had no proof. It would be a very watery accusation that would quickly evaporate.

Avery could say something, obviously, as could his mother, but Amy didn't believe either would. There was no value in destroying their own reputations, and Amy's parents were equally determined to keep it a private matter. Her mother much preferred to use it as salt in Amy's wounds, dropping it as an aside to blame Amy for her own tribulations like being dumped by her latest paramour.

That would let up once she realized Amy was still seeing Luca, of course.

There was a bonus! Amy paused the hair dryer to drink in a fantasy of her mother groveling for an invitation to meet Amy's beau, once she believed her daughter had a real future with royalty.

Which she didn't. Amy's soaring heart took a nosedive. Even if they slept together again, their relationship was still about optics. Nothing more.

She ignored the streak of loss that cut through her chest and returned to yanking the brush through her hair as she dried it, ruthlessly scraping the bristles across her scalp as an exercise in staying real.

Luca wasn't a sociopathic lothario like Avery, but he was a man. The wires between heart and hard-on weren't directly connected. No matter what she did, she had to protect her own heart so it might be better if she and Luca only pretended to be involved.

She didn't want to pretend, she acknowledged with a twist of remorse wrapped in wicked anticipation. Despite the fact that sleeping with him had pulled the rug out from under her hard enough to topple her entire life, she wanted to make love with him again. She wanted to run her hands across his flexing back, feel his lips against her skin. Play her tongue against his and lose herself to the grind of his hips—

Whew! Had the AC cut out? She fanned her cheeks and opened the door to let the humidity out of the bathroom.

Fabiana was packing the clothing that didn't belong to her into a suitcase that was also not hers. "The prince will be ready to travel shortly. He asks that you join him at the helipad in one hour? I've set out your lunch."

A few hours later, Amy was in Milan's fashion district, enjoying a crisp white wine with bruschetta. Luca was beside her, speaking Italian into his phone.

"That looks like it would suit you," he said as he ended his call and pocketed his phone. He nodded at the model on the catwalk.

"I like the train, but I prefer the neckline on the blue." She pointed at the model posing toward the back. "The gala isn't black tie. Could I wear something like that fade?"

"Wear whatever you want," Luca assured her, picking up her hand and touching his lips to her knuckles. "I'm indulging the woman who has captured my heart. I want the world to know it."

Her own heart flipped and twittered like a drunken bird even as she reminded herself it wasn't real. Nevertheless, she leaned in and cut him a sly look that he would recognize as her rebellious streak coming to the fore if he knew her well enough.

"Anything? Because I would love something very avant-garde."

Luca's indulgent nod said, *By all means.* "Control the narrative. Tell them what to talk about."

Amy looked to the designer. "What do you have that says, 'space opera'?"

The woman lit up with excitement and rushed into the back with her models.

Soon Amy was being fitted for a dress that hugged her curves while stiff, saucer-like ruffles gave the impression of a stack of dishes about to fall. The glittering sequins reflected prisms in every direction and a matching hat with a polka dot veil completed the dramatic look.

When she was back in her own clothes, she came upon Luca saying something about Vallia to an attendant. Parcels were being taken to the car.

"That's casual wear for the island," he said. "The rest will be sent to Vallia with the gown for our other events."

"What other events?"

"Cocktail parties. Ribbon cuttings. I'm making an award presentation in Tokyo after the gala."

Then what? There was a small cloud of anxiety chasing her. She had a career to get back to, and she had never aspired to be any man's mistress. She'd cleared a block of time to work with Luca so she still had a few days to consider all her options, but no matter if she only pretended or was really his lover, it wouldn't last.

They left the design house, but word had leaked that they were in Milan. They were chased back to the helicopter, soon landing on a blessedly remote and quiet island.

They disembarked into what could only be described as a fairy-tale setting. A wall of craggy, inhospitable mountains plunged down to the jewel-blue lake. A quaint village sat on the far shoreline. A handful of boats dragged skiers in their wake, keeping their distance.

Luca told her the castle had been built as a monastery in the fifth century. It had a tall, square bell tower in the middle of one outer wall, but the rest was only three stories. The ancient stone walls were covered in moss and ivy. A pebbled pathway led them from the helipad, winding beneath boughs that smelled of Christmas pine and fresh earth and summer vacation.

"No vehicles, just a golf cart for the luggage and groceries by boat," Luca said, pointing into a man-made lagoon surrounded by stone walls as they passed. Two fancy looking speedboats were moored there alongside a utilitarian one that was being unloaded.

They entered through what had once been a scullery room. It was now a very smart if casual entryway with hooks for their jackets and a box bench where they left their shoes.

This was why he called it a cottage, she supposed. It was homey and he exchanged a friendly greeting with the chef as they passed the kitchen, nodding approval for whatever menu was suggested.

"The sun is beginning to set. He asked if we wanted to eat something while we watch it from the terrace or view it from the top of the tower?"

"The tower sounds nice."

He relayed her preference, and they climbed to the belfry where no bell hung.

"I have no plans to ring it, so why replace it?" he said as he led her up a heart-stoppingly narrow spiral of stairs that took them to the roof. "This has been inspected. We're safe," he assured her.

"I forgot my phone," she said with a pat of her pockets. "I want photos!"

She went to the corners of the roof, more awed by the view each direction she looked. She paused to watch where the sun was sinking behind one peak, leaving a glow of gold across the surrounding mountaintops. The air was clean and cool, the height dizzying enough to make her laugh.

"You must have loved coming here as a child. How long has it been in your family?"

"I bought it for myself when it came on the market a few years ago."

"Oh. That's interesting." She glanced at him. "Why?"

"Because it's beautiful and private." His tone said, *Obviously.*

"You didn't buy it to hide your women here?"

"Like a dragon with a damsel? Yes, I've lured you here and you can't leave until your hair grows long enough to climb down. No, Amy. What women are you even talking about?"

"I don't know. The ones you have affairs with. Discreetly. On private islands." She turned to the view because this was a conversation they had to have, but she didn't know how.

"Actually, this is where I hide from those legions of women, to rest and regain my virility," he said dryly. "I've allowed my sister to stay here, but you're the only person I've brought as my guest, female or otherwise."

"Ever?" She moved to another corner.

"Why is that so surprising? Exactly how many lovers do you think I've had?"

"Enough to get really good at sex," she said over

her shoulder, as if she didn't care. She did care. A lot more than she ought to.

"*You're* really good at sex." He came up behind her to trace his fingertips in a line down her back. "Should I ask how many men you've been with?"

"How do you know it's just men?" She swung around and threw back her head in challenge.

He didn't laugh. Or take her seriously.

"You really do have to work harder to shock me," he admonished. "I honestly don't care what you've done or with whom so long as it was consensual and safe enough that I don't have to worry about my own health."

Her heart faltered. She wondered if she could shock him with the deplorable thing she'd done with her teacher, but he set his hands on the wall on either side of her waist, crowding her into the corner. Now all she could see was his mouth, and her thoughts scattered.

"I'm *very* interested in what sort of history you'd *like* to have. With me. What do you want to do, Amy?"

"Nothing kinky," she warned, reflexively touching his chest. "Just normal things."

"Normal?" His smile was wide, but bemused. "Like tennis and jigsaw puzzles?"

"Yes," she said pertly. "And read books to one another. Austen preferably, but I'll allow some Dickens so long as we have a safe word."

"*Nicholas Nickleby?*" The corners of his mouth

deepened. "Tease. Will you sleep in my bed and continue to ruin me for every other woman alive?"

It was flirty nonsense. Banter. But she was incredibly sensitive to words like "ruin."

She swallowed. "I don't want to be your downfall, Luca. I don't want…"

He sobered and brushed a wisp of hair away from her cheek. "What?"

She didn't want to get hurt. Not again.

"I don't want to get confused about what this is." She touched a button on his shirt. "It's just an affair. Right? For a couple of weeks? To, um, take the worst of the poison out of what's going on out there?" She jerked her chin toward the world at large.

He backed off, equally somber. "We barely know each other," he reminded her. "I'm not saying I don't take this seriously, but I can't promise anything permanent. I've never had the luxury of contemplating a future with anyone. Marriage has always been something I would undertake with a woman vetted by a team of palace advisers." His mouth twisted and he dropped his hands to his sides, fully stepping away. "I still have to think that way until Sofia marries and produces our next ruler."

"So you're offering an affair." She hugged herself. "That's fine, but I need to be clear on what to expect since we'll be pretending it's…more."

After a long moment, he gave a jerky nod. "Yes," he agreed. "Just an affair."

And wasn't that romantic.

She looked to where the sun had set and the sky was fading. The glow of excitement inside her had dimmed and dulled, too.

"We should go down while we still have light," she suggested, more to pivot from how bereft she suddenly felt.

He looked as though he wanted to say something, but stifled it and nodded.

He went in front of her, promising to catch her if she missed a foot on the narrow, uneven steps. It was dizzying and nerve-racking, and she clung tightly to the rope that was strung through iron rings mounted to the wall, thinking the whole time, *Don't fall, don't fall.*

But she feared she probably would.

CHAPTER NINE

LUCA WAS RESTLESS and prickly. He blamed the fact he was at a crossroads, having given up the throne, but not yet having found his place in the new order. The work that typically dominated his thoughts now fell to his sister, and the mental vacuum allowed him to dwell on the public's reaction to his fall from grace.

And the woman who had caused it.

They weren't dressing for dinner, but Amy had disappeared to call her business partners, leaving him to nurse a drink and contemplate how completely she seemed to have shut down once he'd pronounced that this was only an affair.

Did she want it to be more? Did he?

He felt as though he'd disappointed her with his answer. Hurt her. That frustrated him. He'd been as honest as possible. Up until that moment, she'd been her bright and funny self. An amusing companion who made him feel alive in ways he had never experienced.

Damn but that was a lot of feelings. He didn't do feelings. They were messy and tended to create the sort of disaster he'd been scrupulously trained to avoid. He'd accomplished what he wanted by giving in to his lust for Amy, but it was time to go back to being his circumspect, disciplined self.

Which meant he shouldn't have a real affair with her, but the mere thought of denying himself when she was willing caused a host of feelings that were more like a swarm of hornets inside him. Which was exactly why he shouldn't indulge—

He swore aloud and set aside his drink as though he could set aside his brooding as easily. Filtering through his texts and emails, he picked up one from an old friend, Emiliano. They had met through their shared interest in emerging tech. Emiliano had since increased his family's fortune by developing tools for facial recognition software.

News bulletin says you're in Milan? I'm at my villa on Lago di Guarda. Join me if you want to escape the fray.

His villa was a comfortable and well-guarded compound.

Luca texted back.

Grazie. We're fine, but I'll be in touch about the solar tiles we discussed last year.

Luca moved on, but Emiliano promptly texted back.

Sounds good. The invitation is open anytime. Tell Amy I said hello.

Just like that, Luca's agitation turned to a ferocious swarm of stinging jealousy.

Jealousy was the most childish of all emotions, but he was bothered and even more bothered by the fact he was bothered. He was having feelings about his feelings, and it was annoying as hell.

Amy returned wearing a concerned frown.

"Is everything all right?" he made himself ask, trying to overcome his sudden possessiveness.

"Clare's overseas and Bea has gone off with a client," she said with a perplexed shake of her head. "When we talked her into joining us, it was purely for legal support, but she got roped into working directly with Ares Lykaios. You would have seen his name on our website. He's our biggest client. We owe him for putting us on the map."

"I know who he is." And there was no reason Luca should feel so threatened that he would ask, "Would you rather be in her place right now?" He hated himself for it.

"A little. Bea must be out of her depth. He's tough and assertive, and Bea's shy by nature. It's always been our dynamic that she helps me work through my internal rubbish and I play her wingman in the external world. She might not know how to handle Ares."

"But you do?"

Her air of distraction evaporated and she narrowed her attention onto him. "He's a client whose professional needs dovetail with the services I offer. Why? What are you suggesting?"

"Nothing," he muttered, disgusted with himself.

"You meant something," she accused. "I don't have personal relationships with clients, Luca. That's why you no longer are one."

"Is Emiliano Ricci a client? Is that how you know him?"

Her expression blanked with surprise, then she shrugged. "Not that it's any of your business, but no. He's not. Why? You said you didn't care what I'd done or with whom."

"I don't," Luca insisted, pacing the lounge. "You were lovers, though?"

"I met him on a weekend cruise for app developers. We talked about social media and how to play the algorithms to become an influencer. I think I'd rather return my mother's phone call than continue *this* conversation."

He let her walk out. He told himself to let her go, to hold himself at a necessary distance. His feelings were too strong as it was. But the farther away she got, the more he knew he was totally blowing this.

"Amy," he called from the bottom of the main staircase.

She paused at the top to give him a haughty look from the rail.

"I don't *want* to care—" he bit out what felt like an enormous confession "—but I do."

"Good for you. I don't." She sailed along the gallery.

The hell she didn't! He took the stairs two at a

time and opened the door to the guest bedroom that she had just slammed in his face.

She swung around to glare at him.

"I don't like having emotions I can't control," he said through his gritted teeth. "Perhaps I should ask your friend Bea to help me work through them?"

Such outraged hostility flashed in her bright green eyes, he nearly threw his head back and laughed. "See? You don't like it, either."

She folded her arms, chin up. "You chased me all the way up here to see if you could make me as pointlessly jealous as you are?"

"I'm not proud of it." He closed in on her. "But I needed to know whether you were capable of it."

"Jealousy comes from insecurity. I'm not an insecure person." She narrowed her eyes and held her ground. Temper crackled around her. She resisted his attempt to unfold her arms.

"Neither am I." He managed to draw her stiff arms open and kissed the inside of each of her blue-veined wrists. "But we haven't had time to become confident in each other, have we? So we're failing the test."

"You specifically told me not to believe in this!" She freed a hand to fling it out with exasperation. "You're the one who said it was a meaningless affair."

"I never said meaningless."

She tried to pull her arm away, but he held on to her wrist. Her struggle drew her closer. Her nose was even with his chin, her gaze wide and surprisingly defenseless beneath the sparks of anger.

That vulnerability dug into him the way her temper and his own conflicting emotions hadn't. He drew her in with great care, twining her one arm behind his lower back, then massaged her stiff shoulders.

"I've always known exactly what was expected of me," he said. "And I've always met and exceeded those expectations." His lips were tickled by flyaway strands of her hair. "But from the moment I met you, I have been off-center. I know what I should be thinking and saying and doing, but I can't make myself do it. Every instinct in me wants to *have* you." His arms tightened around her. "But I can't let that animal win. Not when I know how dangerous it is. The war inside me is killing me so you'll have to forgive the snarls." He ran his hand into her lower back.

It took a few circles of his palm before she released a noise that landed somewhere between defeat and petulance.

"This is new for me, too. From the job you hired me for to how I react to you…" She picked one of her red-gold hairs off his sleeve, then rested her hand where it had been. "I'm not being coy. This is hard to navigate."

"I know. I've made it hard. You have a right to be angry with me, which makes me less sure of you." He let one hand settle above her tailbone.

"I'm not angry or blaming you." Her brow pulled

with consternation. "I took the job and slept with you. I caused us to be seen. I know how much of this is on me and that's hard, too. I'm worried about how our efforts to turn this around will pan out."

"It's going to be harder if we're fighting, no?"

"Whose fault is that?" she admonished, but grew pliant, leaning her thighs against his.

"Guilty." He let his fingers fan out to graze the upper curve of her backside. "Maybe we should kiss and make up. For the sake of our image."

"Humph." Her lips twitched. "Here in the privacy of this bedroom? Where no one can see us? A strong brand has to be reinforced consistently."

"Ooh. More shop talk, *amata mia*." He nuzzled his mouth into her throat, groaning with mock lust. "It makes me so hot."

She laughed and tried to shrug away from his tickling kiss. "Does it? Because I was going to say that I'm currently with the only man who interests me, but okay. Let me tell you about shareable infographics."

He lifted his head, accosted by the most intense flush of pleasure. The kind that should have had an orgasm as its source. And yes, he hoped to experience one of those very soon, but this was even more deeply affecting because it wasn't a biological reaction. It was an expansive, chaotic and thrilling reaction to a throwaway remark she had buried in nonsensical teasing. It was terrifying how much it meant to him.

"What?" she asked, smile faltering.

"Nothing." He cupped her cheek and set his mouth across hers, the avaricious beast in him howling to consume her, but something soft and equally ravenous urged him to be tender. To savor as he plundered. To pour himself into her even as he felt her start of surprise and tasted her broken sigh of capitulation.

Amy had been confused after their rooftop discussion, coming away wondering if she was allowing herself to be used again. She had wanted desperately to reach out to her friends to start putting all of this into perspective.

Neither had been available and for a few minutes, when she'd come back to the lounge, things between her and Luca had seemed to devolve into chaos. She had stalked up here insulted and filled with misgivings and now...

Now she was more confused than ever.

If he was using her, it was in the most tender way possible. His kiss was fierce and insatiable and shatteringly gentle. He was treating her like she was precious and irresistible. He unraveled her ability to think clear thoughts.

She knew nothing but her body and the feel of him where he touched her. The fingerprints he traced on her cheeks near her ear, the playful scrape of his teeth on her bottom lip, the brush of his thighs against hers and the wonderous way he cradled her breast.

The onslaught wasn't only physical. There was tremendous emotion welling in her as she heard his muted groan ring in his chest. She thrilled to the press of his erection into her middle and sighed with adoration when he touched his lips to her brow.

And she trembled. It was nearly too much, the way he made her feel so beautiful and treasured at once. The way he had shared his struggle. She felt it in the brief bite of his fingertips into her hips before he slowly eased her clothing away. Tasted it like whiskey on his tongue when he made love to her mouth before he kissed the nipples he'd exposed and slowly, erotically, made her writhe with need by sucking on them.

"Luca," she gasped.

His eyes were incandescent as he backed her toward the bed. Then he was over her, both of them with their clothing askew, but neither was willing to break apart to undress completely.

"I need you to take me inside you. I need that like I need air to breathe," he said, making her shiver.

With damp eyes, she nodded, needing it too. Needing the physical closeness to seal the schism that had been wrought by the betraying photo and everything that had come after.

Moments later, he had sheathed himself and, both still half-dressed, disheveled and frantic, they came together with a shudder of grand surrender to the passion they couldn't resist.

He held himself inside her as he brushed her hair from where it was caught on her eyelashes. She turned her mouth into the flexing curve of his biceps, tasting his skin and feeling drunk.

"I don't know if I'll ever be able to live without this." As the words left her, she realized she had spoken them aloud.

She saw the beast then. Caught the flash of feral possessiveness before his mouth was at the corner of hers, soft and tender and sweet again.

"Be with me now," he commanded.

He began to move. She had no choice but to lose herself to the exaltation that was the result of their lovemaking. The pleasure lifted her even as it seemed to strip her of any outer, protective layers, until she was nothing but pure being. Pure reaction.

Undone and completely vulnerable.

But he took care of her. Such care. Drawing her to the peak with those kisses of reverence and blatant hunger. Watching her with such pride and pleasure in her joyous ascent to climax.

"I want you with me," she gasped.

"I'm right here." His voice seemed to speak inside her head, they were so attuned.

And then they were splintering together, writhing and groaning and throbbing in perfectly synchronized culmination.

It was so powerful and magnificent, she couldn't open her eyes after. She stayed in that state of mutual bliss for ages, convinced they were actually one being.

"That was incredible," he whispered when they finally disengaged. He discarded the condom and they shifted to a more comfortable position. His fingers sifted through her hair then settled against her scalp, tangled in the strands. "Green-eyed monster slayed. I was a fool to think any man from your past could have any bearing on what we have."

His words should have been reassuring, but her eyes snapped open as one particular man from her past jumped into her head.

It wouldn't come out, she assured herself, while clammy fingers of apprehension squeezed her lungs. Was she being naive? Forewarned was forearmed. She ought to tell him.

It was so shameful, though. She hated to even recollect it. Trying to explain it, to dredge through the guilt and remorse and betrayal by her parents... His view of her would completely change. She didn't want to ruin this newfound closeness between them. Not right now.

His chest rose and fell beneath her ear as he exhaled into sleep. She snuggled closer and let unpleasant memories drift away.

"How does it feel to no longer be the most noteworthy person in the room?" Luca's twin asked as she appeared beside him.

Queen Sofia of Vallia was the height of elegance in one of their mother's vintage gowns and a tiara from the crown jewel collection. Her attendance at the foundation's gala was her first public event and their first appearance together since La Inversione, as the press had dubbed her bloodless coup.

Luca noted his sister's gaze was on Amy where she swiveled for the relentlessly flashing bulbs around her. Was Sofia criticizing the attention Amy was garnering? A twist of hostility wrenched through him aimed at the one person he'd always vowed to lay down his life to protect.

He sipped his drink, dampening his desire to remind her that she had been elevated to her current position at Amy's expense. "I never wanted to be. You know that."

"I was teasing." Her gaze narrowed at his tone. "You like her."

Which made him realize he was overreacting, damn it.

"I don't sleep with people I don't like," he muttered.

"Obviously. But you *really* like her. I was under the impression this was all for my benefit," she mused, looking back at Amy with consideration.

He took another gulp of his drink, guilty because this wasn't supposed to benefit him at all. Nothing was. Ever. He hadn't saddled Sofia with running their country so he could enjoy a sexual romp.

"I'll invite her to lunch," Sofia said. "Get to know her better."

"She's due back in London as soon as we return from Tokyo."

Her steady gaze asked, *And then what?*

He rubbed his thumb against the side of his glass, not ready to admit he was thinking of going there with her. There were so many variables and pitfalls. Sofia wasn't married or even looking for a consort. The public might be *for* Queen Sofia, but many were still taking sides *against* Amy Miller for costing them King Luca.

"She handles it well, doesn't she? Being in the sun," Sofia mused.

Amy was winning people over one bright smile at a time, but the attention would never stop. Nor would the judging. It was a sad and relentless fact of his life that he had to remain above reproach. He couldn't sentence her to those same strictures. Not forever.

Not when her smile was already showing signs of strain.

"Yes, but she's not wearing sunscreen." He set his glass on a drinks tray carried by passing waitstaff. "Excuse me while I rescue her."

Amy gratefully went into Luca's arms when he invited her to dance.

"How are you holding up?" he asked as he led her into a smooth waltz. Was there *nothing* this man didn't do perfectly?

"I underestimated what I was asking of my clients in the past, when I've said, 'Just smile while they take your photo.' My fault, I guess, for choosing this dress."

His expression flickered through amusement and

ended up as something more contemplative. "There's a commentary there on how much attention we give to what women wear, but I'd rather not think too hard when I've finally got you to myself."

"I'll wear a tuxedo next year," she said, then faltered as she realized it sounded like she assumed she would be with him next year.

"Or pajamas," he suggested.

She relaxed. "I'm glad they've been well received, but I can't take the credit."

"Why not? Sofia and I wouldn't have ordered any if the option hadn't been presented."

Even so, the queen and former king had each preordered a hundred pair, asking that they be donated to long-term care facilities throughout Vallia. With that example set, guests were ordering in factors of ten, rather than the one or two pair Amy had anticipated.

"Do you want to visit the pajama factory while we're in Asia?" Luca asked.

"Oh. Um…" She nearly turned her ankle again. "While you're doing that award thing in Tokyo? I mean, yes. I'd love to connect with the manufacturer and be sure it's a fair wage factory, like they claim. Double-check the quality."

"Get a photo op? We'll go together."

"Look at you, doing my job for me."

"I'm in the midst of a career change. Willing to try new things."

She chuckled, more from happiness than humor,

but he made her *so* happy. Glowingly, deliriously lighthearted and hopeful and filled with a sense that she was the luckiest person alive. Especially when his gaze swung down to connect with hers, conveying pride and sexy heat.

This optimism was strange because she had learned the hard way not to look to a man to make her happy. She knew it had to come from within, but even though she would have said she was very content prior to meeting Luca, she felt far more alive and excited now that she was with him. Colors were brighter, music more tear-inducing, her confidence unshakable.

She wondered if this was what being in love felt like—

Oh.

He steadied her, pausing to give her a small frown. "How much have you had to drink?"

"One glass. I was just…distracted for a moment," she lied.

They resumed dancing, but her whole body was fizzing with the realization that her heart had gift wrapped itself and stolen under his tree.

She was in love with him. How it had happened so quickly didn't matter. It had. Because this wasn't a hero-worship crush gone wrong. Or sexual infatuation—although that was definitely a big part of it.

It was deep concern for his well-being. Admiration for his principles and intelligence and laconic wit. It was a compulsion to trust him with all of her secrets and a depthless yearning for him to return her regard.

The words clogged her throat, but it was too soon. Too public. Too new.

But as they continued dancing, she thought it with each step.

I love you. I love you.

The next days were busy.

Luca was in meetings to redefine his new role and Amy worked remotely, attempting to mitigate the damage her scandal had done to London Connection and her career.

She rarely had Luca to herself, and when she did, it was in bed. There they communicated in ways that were as profound as any conversation she might have wished to have, so she didn't worry that they weren't dissecting their relationship. It was growing stronger by the day.

The unrelenting media pressure only pushed them to rely on one another, rather than rending them apart. If an awkward question was directed at her, his hand would come out of nowhere to interlace with hers. When his bearing grew rife with tension over a late-night pundit's joke at his expense, she would slide her arms around his waist, asking nothing except that he allow her to soothe him. He would sigh and gather her in.

This morning he had commented to someone, "I'm likely to be in London for the next while—"

It had been part of a broader discussion, and she hadn't had an opportunity to ask if that meant he wanted to continue their relationship. They had agreed on two weeks, but she didn't need to do any soul-searching. Of course, she wanted to keep seeing him!

They were both in love. She was sure of it. If that put a dreamy, smitten look on her face, she couldn't help it.

Perhaps that's why she was garnering so many stares right now.

Or maybe it was because this morning, she and Luca had been granted an exclusive visit to Shinjuku Gyoen National Garden to view their cherry blossoms with some Japanese dignitaries. A handful of photographers had followed them, and those shots were likely being published right now.

Either way, her phone, which was facedown on the table and set to silent, was vibrating incessantly.

She ignored it and kept her attention on Luca. He spoke at the podium, switching back and forth between Italian and Japanese so she missed much of what he was saying. She could tell there was praise for collaboration and innovation on some tech solution commissioned for Vallia. He showed a photo of a port in Vallia, then one here in Japan, highlighting some advancement that had made a difference in both countries.

One of Luca's handlers stood behind him. The young man sent her an urgent glare.

Seriously? He could hear the buzz of her phone all the way over there?

She slid the phone off the table without looking at it and dropped it into her bag.

She had the sense of more glances turning her way, but reminded herself that a few rude stares were a small price to pay for the absolute wonder of being Luca's... They didn't need a label, she assured herself. None of the usual ones fit them anyway. "Girlfriend" was too high school. "Lover" was too edgy for a prince, "mistress" too eye-rollingly outdated.

Luca *had* been footing her bills since she'd met him. Even her charge from the hotel boutique in London had been reversed. Apparently, he'd had the clothes she'd bought that day put onto his own account.

That made her uncomfortable, but she pulled her weight in other ways. She was still managing the pajama campaign and offered constructive ideas to his team on how she and Luca were presenting themselves. They were equals.

Luca came to the good part, announcing a pair of names and the company they represented. Everyone clapped as a husband-wife team rose to collect the statuette Luca held.

The audience took advantage of the applause break to set their heads together and murmur, flicking speculative glances toward her. Luca joined his assistant behind the winners and glanced at the screen his assistant showed him.

He stiffened and his gaze lifted in a flash to hit hers like a punch.

Amy's stomach clenched. *What?*

As the couple at the podium finished speaking and left, they seemed disconcerted by the growing undercurrents in the room.

The cameraman who'd been filming the event turned his lens on her. A reporter shoved a microphone in Amy's face.

"Is it true? Did you cause a teacher to lose his position with Upper Swell School for Girls? Do you have a history of destroying men's lives?"

CHAPTER TEN

LUCA DISAPPEARED OFF the stage behind the curtain, abandoning her to the reckoning of harsh stares and harsher questions.

As Amy was absorbing the profound pain of his desertion, another reporter joined the first. People stared while she desperately tried to gather her handbag and light jacket, which was being pinned by a reporter. On purpose.

Panic began to compress her lungs. She struggled to maintain her composure. She was hot and cold and *scared*. As scared as she'd been the day she was told to leave the school and had no idea where she would go.

Do not cry. Do not, she willed herself while her throat closed over a distressed scream.

And these damned buzzards kept asking their cruel questions.

"Did you lure the prince into that nude photograph? Did someone hire you to do it? His sister?"

One of Luca's bodyguards shoved into the fray

and shielded her with his wide body and merciless bulk. He grabbed her things and escorted her out of the nearest exit, but it was still a gauntlet of shouted questions and conjecture.

When he shoved her into an SUV, Luca was already in it. His PA sat facing him; his other bodyguard was in the front. The bodyguard who had rescued her took the seat facing her and pulled the door shut behind them.

"Is it true?" Luca asked stiffly. She hadn't seen this particular shade of subdued rage under his skin since he'd spoken of his father's death.

"I'm not talking about it here." Her voice was hollow. All of her was. It was the only way she could cope, by stepping outside her body and letting the shell be transported wherever he was taking her. If she let herself see and think and feel, she would buckle into hysterical tears.

"That's not a denial," he growled.

How had this happened? Why?

"Who—" She had to clear the thickness from her throat so her voice was loud enough to catch the PA's attention. "Who released this story?"

He told her the name of an infamous gossip site. "Their source is the wife of Avery Mason. She claims he confided in her early in their marriage."

Amy set her hand across her aching stomach and looked out the window.

"The flight plan has been changed, sir," Luca's

PA informed him after tapping his tablet. "The team will meet us when we refuel in Athens."

No photo op at a factory in Jiangsu then. Big surprise. "The team" would be the same group of lawyers, spin doctors and palace advisers who had handled his first damning scandal and were continuing to massage it.

Obviously, *she* was off the job. Amy couldn't be trusted. Luca would control the messaging, and his lawyers would likely press her to sign something. Maybe Luca would sue her for defamation. The contract she'd signed with him hadn't stated explicitly that she was supposed to ruin him. They'd left that part as a handshake deal. Could that come back to bite her? She needed Bea!

The private airfield came into view. They drove up to his private jet, and even that short walk of shame was photographed from some hidden location that turned up on her phone when she checked it as the plane readied for takeoff.

"You're shaking," Luca said crisply. "Do you need something?"

A time machine? Her friends? She dug up one of the sleeping tablets she'd taken on the flight here, requested a glass of water and swallowed the pill.

Luca answered a call and began speaking Italian. His sister perhaps. He was cutting his words off like he was chopping wood. Or beheading chickens.

"Sì. No lo so. Presto. Addio."

She handed back her glass and texted Bea and

Clare, already knowing it was futile. They were tied up with other things, and she didn't know how to ask for forgiveness when she was piling yet more scandal onto London Connection.

In a fit of desperation, she sent out a text to a few of her closest contacts, fearful she would be locked down in Vallia again. A commercial flight was out of the question. She'd be torn apart, but a handful of her clients flew privately throughout Europe. There was a small chance one of them might be going through the airfield Luca used in Athens.

As she was texting, her mother's image appeared on her screen as an incoming call.

Don't cry. Do not cry.

Amy hit ignore, then tapped out a text that she was about to take off and had to set her phone to airplane mode. It wasn't true, but she couldn't face the barrage that was liable to hit her. She turned off her phone and set it aside.

Luca tucked away his own phone and studied her.

The plane began to taxi. The flight attendant had seated herself near the galley. The rest of his staff were sequestered in their own area, leaving them alone in this lounge, facing one another like duelists across twelve paces of tainted honor.

"Yes. It's true," she said flatly, appreciating the cocooning effect of her sleeping tablet as it began to release into her system, reducing her agitation and making her limbs feel heavy. It numbed her to the profound humiliation of reliving the most agonizing, isolating experience of her life. "I had an affair with my teacher in my last year of school. That's why I was expelled and why my parents disinherited me."

"How old was he?"

"Twenty-nine. I was eighteen."

He swore. "That's not an affair, Amy. He should have been arrested."

"Oh, he's a disgusting pig. I won't argue that, but I came on to him, even after he said we shouldn't. I told you I was spoiled. I wasn't used to taking no for an answer. I loved how enamored with me he seemed. How helpless he was to resist me."

She saw how deeply that hit Luca, pushing him back into his seat. Making him reconsider his own infatuation with her.

Was she *trying* to hurt him with this chunk of heavy, sharp-edged history? Maybe. Kicking it at him felt like the only way she could handle touching it at all.

"I'd never had to face any consequences before that. If I was caught bringing alcohol into the dorm, my parents would make a donation to the school and smooth things over." That had been her father's solution, to avoid a fight with his ex over which one of them had to bring Amy back into their home. "I was friends with everyone. It was a point of pride that even if someone thought I was full of myself, I would win them over by flattering them and doing them favors." That had been her mother's legacy. If you didn't have a clear pressure point like money or maternal guilt to bring to bear, fawning and subtle bribery were good substitutes. "I refused to let up when he tried to turn me down."

"Grown men are not victims of teenage girls," he said with disgust.

"Not until his mother, the headmistress, discovers them. Then he's apparently a defenseless baby and the harlot who seduced him is served with an overdue notice of expulsion. *That's* when her parents finally decide she should be taught a lesson about the real world."

His flinty gaze tracked across her expression.

It was all she could do to hide how devastated she'd been. Still was. She looked away, out the window to where Tokyo was fading behind wisps of cloud.

A tremendous melancholy settled on her. The sleeping pill, but history, as well.

"It was covered up by his mother and mine. The gossip hadn't really got around anyway. Bea and Clare were the only two people who stood by me. They wanted to quit school in solidarity, but I didn't want them to throw away their futures just because I had. They helped with rent here and there, but I eventually found my feet with the online promotions and I was so…touched. So *proud* when Clare asked me to start London Connection with her. I felt like I was bringing value when I'd been such a mess in those early years. And now… Now I've stuffed it up anyway."

"Why did you take my assignment when you had something like this in your past?"

"I didn't expect to *relive* it. You're the one who decided to use me for your own ends because the opportunity was too good to pass up," she reminded him.

His head jerked back. "I would have made other decisions if I had known."

"Would you?" she scoffed.

"You didn't give me a chance to prove otherwise, did you? I came to you to manufacture a scandal so I wouldn't cause anyone else to be hurt. *I told you that*. But you didn't warn me that something like this was possible. You said this is a circle of trust, but you didn't trust me, did you?"

"Don't lecture me on *honesty*. Not when you—" She leaned forward in accusation, then abruptly had to catch her armrest as she realized the tablet was destroying her sense of balance. "When you were so convinced of your own perfection you had to *hire* someone to make you look bad. You want to talk about respecting a relationship? You hired me so that when you made your *one* mistake—" she showed him her single finger for emphasis "—it wouldn't really be yours. You wanted to be able to tell yourself that whatever happened wouldn't really be your fault. You want to believe this image—" she gestured to encompass his aura "—of being completely flawless, is *real*. Here's news, Luca. We all make mistakes. That's why my job exists! I'm *your* mistake. And now you'll have to live with that. So suck it."

She dropped back into her seat, feeling like a sack of bruised apples. The entire world was upon her, crushing her. She propped her cement-filled head on the weak joint of her wrist, growing too tired to cry, even though sobs were thickening her throat and sinuses.

"My mistake was believing the scarlet harlot of Upper Swell was going to live happily ever after with the Golden Prince."

"I never promised you that." He didn't shout it, but it struck like a sonic boom she felt with her heart.

"No," she agreed with growing drowsiness. "No, you said it was only going to be an affair and I believed you. But you made me fall in love with you." She blinked heavy lids over wet eyes. "That's on you, Luca."

Amy woke in Luca's stateroom several hours later. She wondered if he had carried her here or had one of his bodyguards do it. Whoever it was had removed her shoes and draped a light blanket over her.

She finger-combed her hair and used the toothbrush that had been designated hers when they'd embarked from Vallia, back when she and Luca had been in perfect sync and she'd believed...

She clenched her eyes. Had she really believed they had a chance at a future? *Come on, Amy. You're smarter than that.*

Wrinkled and fuzzy-headed, she crept back to her seat.

Luca was reclined in his seat and fast asleep. Her heart wrenched to see him there when he could have slept beside her in his own bed. If he had wanted to send the message that she would no longer wake to the sight of him sleeping beside her, this was it.

A flight attendant started to approach, and Amy waved her off. She should eat something so she didn't get air sick, but she was too anguished.

She turned on her phone and was tempted to turn it right back off again, but made herself go through some of the messages, looking for...

Her heart lurched as she picked up a reply to her SOS. One of her clients, Baz Rivets, was sober a year now, but had had addiction problems from the time she'd met him at one of his early pub gigs through to the international fame he and his rock band enjoyed today. She'd been beside him every time he'd gone in or come out of a program and regarded him as a friend, but she would never have expected him to go out of his way for her.

I thought I'd have to go back to rehab to see you again. We're detouring to Athens from Berlin. Will wait for you there, ducky.

It was enormously heartening, but also like hearing she could have lifesaving surgery on condition half her heart be removed.

With her throat aching, she replied with a heartfelt, "Thank you," and set aside her phone. Then she stared at the flight tracker, taking way too long to comprehend that they were above Turkey. Only a few hours to go before she would have to say goodbye to Luca.

He woke as they began their descent into Athens.

For one millisecond, as he glanced at her with disorientation, she saw a flash of the complex *hello* he usually wore when he woke next to her. It was discovery and pleasure and something magnetic and welcoming that always warmed her deep in her center.

This time, it was gone before it fully formed. She saw memory strike him so hard, he flinched. His expression blanked into steely, unreadable lines.

Whatever spark of hope still flickered within her died, leaving her more bereft than she'd ever felt. She looked to the window, teeth clenched against making apologies. Was this her fault? Not really. Everyone had a past, and she hadn't aired hers on purpose.

Did that matter when it was impacting him anyway? Her parents hadn't cared who was at fault ten years ago. *This can't get out, Amy. How did you let it happen?*

Her ears popped and, moments later, they were on the ground, taxiing to a stop outside a private terminal for personal and charter jets.

"I have to speak with my sister," Luca said, glancing up from his ringing phone. He unbuckled and rose, bringing the phone to his ear as he moved into the stateroom for privacy.

Amy searched wildly out the window as she began gathering her things. A team of trench coats and briefcases came out of the terminal and headed toward the plane. Fresh air came in as the steps were lowered.

Where was Baz? There! She saw the plane with the psychedelic logo on its tail and rudely shuffled her way past the confused faces of people trying to board.

It was raining and she hadn't bothered to pull on her light jacket, so she felt each stinging drop as she ran the short distance across the tarmac. Stairs appeared as the hatch was lowered on Baz Rivets's plane.

"Welcome to the naughty side, ducky!" Baz wore jeans, a torn T-shirt, a man bun and a scruffy beard. He opened his arms in welcome.

She ran up the steps, starting to cry, she was so overwhelmed. "I didn't know how to get home without being swarmed, but I didn't expect you to make a special trip for me!"

"You flew to Thailand and kept me out of *jail*. Giving you a lift home is the least I can do." He wrapped his arms around her. "You messy, messy girl."

"I never claimed to be otherwise, Baz. I really didn't."

"Oh. He doesn't look happy."

Amy turned to see Luca had come onto the steps of his own plane. He stared across at her, his dumbfounded rage so tangible she felt a jolt of adrenaline sear her arteries.

Baz kept one arm around her and drew her closer

to his wiry frame. He wore the most neighborly of smiles as he waved and spoke with quiet cheerfulness through his clenched teeth, "That'll teach you, ya royal bastard. Amy should be treated like the queen she is."

I'm not. I was never going to be.

For a long moment, she and Luca stared at one another. He didn't call her back or come get her, though. And he turned away first.

It was a knife straight to her heart, one that would have kept her standing there waiting for the rest of her life in hopes he'd reappear to pull it out, but Baz nudged her inside.

"Come tell Uncle Bazzie all about it. Lads, put the kettle on for our sweet Ames."

Luca was clinging to his patience by his fingernails. His brain kept going back to asking *Why didn't she tell me this could happen?*

It didn't matter why. She hadn't. Intellectually, he understood that Amy was the victim of exploitation. That wasn't something she needed to tell anyone unless she wanted to.

But now his sister was in his ear saying, "I appreciate this isn't something she could control, but it's time to distance yourself from her."

"I know." His goal had been accomplished, and Amy's connection to him was making things worse for her.

The woman who had leaked the story wouldn't have been so well rewarded if she'd only been taking down a PR agent who worked with celebrities. No, Amy's romantic link to royalty had been the gold the story was really mining. It was a vein that would continue to be exploited as long as he and Amy were together.

Even so, when Luca saw Amy darting across the tarmac to the waiting plane, he nearly lost his mind.

He'd hung up on his sister and shoved his way outside in time to see her with— Who the hell was that? Some demigod celebrity, Luca realized as he took in the flamboyant logo that spoke of a live fast, die young rock culture. The jackass wore professionally distressed clothing and a smug grin as he claimed Amy.

Luca hated him on sight.

You made me fall in love with you.

If she loved him, she should have trusted him enough to tell him about her past. Enough to *stay.*

That's all he could think as he stared across at her standing in that other man's embrace, the image like radiation that destroyed his insides the longer he stared.

"Sir, there are people in the terminal getting all this on their phones," someone said from inside his plane.

Brilliant. His final humiliation was being recorded for uploading to the buffet of public ignominy that was already so well stocked. Outstanding.

He went inside to take his seat, sick with guilt that he'd wanted to right a wrong and it had resulted in yet more wrong.

Everyone stared at him while he settled into his chair.

"Our first step is to make clear to her the legal and financial consequences she will face if she divulges any of this to the press," one of his lawyers piped up.

"We should make an immediate statement that she was *asked* to leave. Get in front of whatever photos come out from this." Another one tapped the window.

Luca had had the team meet him here in Athens in hopes they could find a way forward that wouldn't destroy both him and Amy. He had expected her to weigh in.

Now he could only stare in disbelief while another backstabbing idiot said, "Given her history, we could reframe the photos and make a case for you to take *back* the throne."

Luca swore and waved his hand. "Get off my plane. All of you."

Neither Bea nor Clare were in London when Amy arrived.

Bea, bless her, said Amy could use her flat. She was deeply grateful and sank into the familiar oasis of Bea's personal space.

But with both of her friends still away, it fell to Amy to keep London Connection running. She popped an email to her assistant to say she would do it remotely to minimize the disruption she was already causing at the office. She didn't mention her plan to resign. She would wait until Clare and Bea were back to tell them personally. For now, she focused on drafting a statement about her past and most recent disgrace.

It started out very remorseful, but the more she looked up statistics on sexual harassment and noted the delight trolls took in being sadistic toward women, and the punishment gap when a woman made a mistake versus a man, the more incensed she became.

She wound up writing:

How is it that a twenty-nine-year-old man was deemed to have more to lose than an eighteen-year-old woman?

Everyone had something to lose when this affair happened, but I—the person with the least life experience and fewest resources—became the scapegoat. I was expelled before I could take my A levels, destroying my university aspirations.

No one cared that my future was derailed. It was far more important to Avery's mother, the headmistress, that she keep her job and avoid a disciplinary hearing over her son's behavior. She convinced my parents to sweep it under the rug. They agreed because they had financial, social, and career pressures to protect.

Instead of urging me to call the police, which I was too humiliated to contemplate on my own, my parents cut me off financially. I was literally left homeless while Avery was immediately transferred to a position at another school.

What began as a PR spin became an essay on feminism and the distance that still needed to be traveled. When she was done, there was morning light outside.

Amy hit send to a senior editor of an old-school but well-respected newspaper in America, then hired bodyguards to escort her to her own flat.

"'The king of Vallia hired me to assist with the Queen's Foundation,'" Sofia read aloud from the same open letter that Luca was reading on his own tablet. "'At the time of my professional engagement, we discussed extending my purview to other assignments, but those discussions were discontinued after we became personally involved.'"

Mio Dio, she knew how to gracefully pirouette with prose, Luca thought.

Perhaps Sofia was thinking it, too. He could feel her staring at him from her position at the opposite end of the table, prodding him for details on those halted discussions.

Luca and his twin had always breakfasted together if they were both in the palace, even after Luca took the throne. It allowed them to connect personally, but also discuss any political developments or other rising concerns. Luca had wanted Sofia to be in the know so she could seamlessly take over when the time came. She was keeping him equally well-informed as a courtesy. She certainly didn't need him

weighing in with advice or opinions. Vallia's popu-
lace was adapting well to the changeover, seeming
energized and eager for the new order.

Luca wished he could say the same. He was mis-
erable.

*While I regret the anguish King Luca must
have suffered from the photos of us that
emerged, I feel no remorse over the fact he
was pressured into giving up the crown as a
result of our affair. Men should be held to account when they cross a line.*

"I like her," Sofia mused.

Me too, Luca thought, heart so heavy in his chest
it was compressed and thumping in rough, painful
beats that echoed in the pit of his gut.

He reached the end where an editorial note stated
that Avery Mason's wife had recently retained an extremely pricey and ruthless divorce lawyer.

"Do you suppose that's why she sold the story?"
Sofia asked as she clicked off her tablet. "To pay for
her divorce?"

"And bolster her petition for one," Luca surmised.
Perhaps she'd seen this as her only avenue for escaping her marriage. He couldn't spare much thought or
empathy for her, though. Not when she'd ruthlessly
used Amy to achieve her own ends.

The way you did? his conscience derided.

"A rebuttal is being drafted," Guillermo said, ever

the helicopter guardian, hovering and batting away threats to his charges.

"Why?" Luca asked. "Do you not think men should suffer the consequences of their actions?"

"Signor." It was one of Guillermo's scolds that backpedaled even as his haughty demeanor reinforced his position. Luca Albizzi was never allowed to be seen as anything but faultless.

You were so convinced of your own perfection you had to hire someone to make you look bad.

"Guillermo, will you leave us please?" Sofia said.

Luca brought his focus back to his sister as Guillermo slipped away.

"I regret nothing," he said, which felt like a lie, but he still waved a dismissing hand at his tablet. "This will pass."

"Luca, I know," Sofia said in a voice that sent a chill of foreboding through him. "About the night Papa died. I made Vincenzo tell me everything." Vincenzo was the head of the palace's legal department.

Luca looked away, instantly thrown back to that grim night. "I was trying to spare you, not hide it from you."

"I know." She rose and came down the length of the table to stand behind him.

He tensed, not wanting comfort. He resisted her touch when her narrow hands settled on his shoulders and she squeezed his set muscles.

"I'm sorry you felt you couldn't tell me. That you've had to carry it alone."

"What was the point in forcing one more ugly memory onto you?"

"I know, but I needed to understand. Something changed in you after that night. At first, I thought it was the pressure of having to ascend. That you were angry the crown hadn't come to me, but it was more than that. I saw it more clearly when you were with Amy. She makes you happy, Luca, but you're fighting that every step of the way. Why?"

"Because look what happens when men in positions of power follow their base instincts!" He waved at the tablet where Amy's words were imprinted for the world to see. "Do you think that would have happened to her if she hadn't been tied to *me*?"

He would have risen to pace, but she didn't let him shrug her off. Her hands pressed him to stay in the chair as if she could impress her views into him with the action.

"You saw how upset she was the day our affair was revealed." He was still haunted by Amy's bleak expression. "She threatened to burn down the palace because she was terrified of exactly *this*."

"You didn't know about it, Luca."

"But I still wouldn't have done anything differently if I had. That's what makes me sick with myself. From the minute I saw her, I wanted her. I was attracted to her and yet I hired her anyway. I brought her here and gave in to what I felt. Pursuing what *I* wanted has destroyed her. So yes, she makes me happy. What the hell can I do about it when I'm a cancer that will only harm her?"

You made me fall in love with you.

He had to breathe through the pain every time he thought about her saying that. In the moment, he'd refused to let it in. His reflex had been to control the damage they faced, but while she'd been sleeping, her words had begun to penetrate and they'd replayed in his head continuously ever since, torturing him. Making him ache with what might have been.

"Do you know why I was away when Papa died?" Sofia asked.

"You were at a UN conference," he recalled dimly.

"The conference was over. I was hiding in a hotel room, worried I was pregnant."

Luca abruptly twisted in his chair to stare up at her.

"It was a false alarm," she hurried to say.

"Who?" he demanded in astonishment.

"Someone who was not anticipating being a father, let alone a queen's consort," she said tartly. "What I'm saying is, you are not the only person who has moments of weakness and fallibility." She cupped his cheek. "You're not the only one who wants to find a life partner and feel loved."

"I will stand behind you no matter what, Sofia. You know that." He took her hand to impress the words into her with a squeeze of her fingers. "You could have told me. If anything like that ever happens again, you can tell me."

"I know. And *I* stand behind *you* no matter what. Despite recent appearances," she said with a quirk of her mouth. Then she waved at his tablet. "Look how strong she is, Luca. Do you really think she's going to let *any* man destroy her? No. She has publicly declared she's keeping the life she has made for herself, and good for her. She is exactly the sort of woman you should be pursuing. She'll keep you honest."

You said it was only going to be an affair and I believed you.

He had tried to believe it himself, but he'd known that every minute with her was more than some flickering memory. It had been a stone in the foundation of something bigger. Something he wanted to make permanent. He'd already been contemplating going to London so they could continue to see one another.

"Do you have any idea how annoying it is that the women in my life are smarter than I am?" He rose.

"At least you're smart enough to realize that."

"Be warned, Sofia. If I'm going after *everything* I want, for me and you and Amy and Vallia, blood may get spilled. I won't always be nice about it."

She smiled. "I've always known you would slay dragons if you were allowed to carry a sword and weren't weighed down by a crown. You've made it possible for me to be who I need to be. I want you to be who *you* were meant to be." She offered her cheek for a kiss. "I love you and trust you."

"*Ti amo, sorella.* Don't wait up. I'll be gone as long as it takes to win her back."

* * *

I was going to resign, but you'll have to fire me.

Amy wrote that to Bea and Clare as she prepared to go into work two days later.

Clare was uncharacteristically silent, not answering texts or emails for the last few days, which was worrying, but Bea called her immediately. "I vote you be promoted to Executive Director of Executing Bastards. You're my hero. I love you."

"Where *are* you? When are you coming back?" Amy asked her.

"It's a lot to explain," Bea began.

"Oh, God. Wait," Amy said as her phone pinged with a text. "My mother is threatening to come see me. I haven't spoken to her since before Tokyo."

"You don't have to see her," Bea reminded her.

"That's what I'm going to tell her." Sort of. "I'll call you back soon." Amy signed off and tapped her mother for a video call.

Her mother looked surprisingly frail, not wearing her usual makeup and designer day dress. Instead, she was in her dressing gown. Her skin looked sallow and aged and, if Amy wasn't mistaken, she was putting out a cigarette off-screen.

"There's a lot of paps outside, Mom. And I'm heading into work so don't come over here. I won't drag them to you, either."

"That's fine, but I *wish* you would have seen all of that old business from my point of view, instead of airing it publicly. In *New York*. Do you have any idea how traumatizing it would have been to put you through a court case over that prat? It was the best thing for you that we made it go away like that. You should be thankful."

"You have a right to your opinion. Is that all?" Amy propped up her phone so she could use two hands to load her bag.

"I've spoken to your father. He's arranging to release your trust fund as soon as possible."

"I don't need it, Mom." She kind of did, but... "I never wanted *money* from you and Dad," she added with a sharp break in her tone that she couldn't help.

"For God's sake, Amy. Have you never realized there was none? It was a recession! Your father borrowed from the trust to keep his company afloat. He stopped paying me support. That's why I married Melvin, so I could sell the house and make your tuition payments. You were adamant that you finished school with your friends. Then you got yourself expelled. I honestly didn't know what to do. We both thought you needed a dose of reality."

"And the reality was, I couldn't count on my parents to be honest with me."

"Do not play the victim here, Amy. You were an absolute pill."

"This is not a productive conversation, Mom. Let's take a break. A long one. I'll call when I'm ready to chat. If you don't hear from me by my birthday, you can call me then."

"In *five months*? No. That stupid Mason fool will not cost me my only child again. I swear, I want to track him down and stab him in the eye."

"Let me know what they set your bail at. I'll see if I can raise it online."

"You think I'm joking."

"You think I am."

"I'll see you at Wednesday's lunch," her mother declared.

Amy rolled her eyes, not caring that it made her mother sigh the way it always had, ever since she'd been a young, rebellious pill.

"I'll text you once I've checked my schedule at work," Amy conceded. "Bea and Clare are away and this is my first day back. It will be hectic."

A short time later, her bodyguards cut through the paparazzi and she entered London Connection. Despite Bea's supportive phone call, however, she wasn't sure of her reception.

"Amy!" someone shouted, and everyone stood up to applaud her.

Which made tears come into her eyes. She was deeply touched and had a queue of hugs to get through before she arrived at her desk and began putting things in order there.

It was a busy day. Some clients had dropped her and the agency, claiming they were "no longer a good fit," but the phones were even busier with potential new ones. Even more heartening were the emails from colleagues in her industry who not only expressed support for her personally, but told her how much they admired her professionally.

"I would rather work for you than the agency I'm at," more than one said. "Please let me know when you have an opening."

As Amy absorbed what an opportunity for growth they faced, she held a quick meeting with the department heads. She tasked them with helping her make a case for expanding London Connection that she could present to Bea and Clare the minute they were back.

It was exciting and consuming and kept her mind occupied so she wouldn't think about how thoroughly her letter had dropped the ax on any chance she might have had of a relationship with Luca. She kept waiting for his rebuttal to hit the airwaves, maybe something that would deride her for daring to be so comfortable with costing a king his crown. The arrogance! The cheek! Did she not know she had destabilized a nation?

There was only a short statement from the palace that they would not comment on the prince's personal life. When she arrived home, however, a pair of stoic-faced men in dark suits were waiting in the lobby of her building.

"Will you come with us, Miss Miller?"

"She will not," one of her own bodyguards said firmly, placing himself in front of her.

"It's fine, I know who he is," she said, nudging her man aside. Her heart began to race and she searched the face of Luca's bodyguard. He gave away nothing.

He probably didn't know what she faced any more than she did.

Would Luca rail at her? Force her to write a retraction? Have her thrown off a bridge?

There was only one way to find out. Despite her trepidation, she dismissed her own guards and went with the men.

They took her to a beautiful Victorian town house in Knightsbridge. The facade was white and ornate. Vines grew up the columns on either side of the black front door. She was shown across a foyer with a lovingly restored parquet floor and into a lounge of predominantly white decor. Three arched windows, tall and narrow and symmetrical, looked onto a garden where a topless maiden poured water from a jug into a fountain.

She looked at the figure and all she could think of was her walk with Luca the first day at his palace, when he'd confided in her about his father's death. He'd been so hurt by the things his father had done, and she'd set him up for more of it.

She rubbed her sternum, hating herself for that.

"It felt like home the minute I saw her," Luca said behind her.

Amy spun to find him leaning in a doorway, regarding her. Her heart leaped a mile high. She had missed him. So much. Then her heart took another bounce because he was so fiercely beautiful. And a third time because there was no anger in his expression. No vilification.

But no smile, either. The one that tugged at her

cheeks fell apart before it was fully formed, but she couldn't help staring at him. Drinking him in.

His neat, stubbled beard was perfectly trimmed across his long cheeks. His mouth was not quite smiling, but wasn't tense, either. Solemn. His blue eyes searched more than they offered any insight to his reason for bringing her here.

He had the ability to wear a blue button-down shirt and gray trousers as though it was a bespoke tuxedo. A suit of gleaming armor. Whether he called himself a king, a prince, or a man, he could lean in a doorway and command a room. He projected authority and strength, and despite his intimidating and unreadable expression and the very unsettled way they'd left things, her instinct was to hurry toward him.

She touched the back of a chair to ground herself. To hold herself back.

They'd been apart only four days. Their relationship from "ruin me" to being ruined had been a short ten. How was it possible that her feelings toward him were paralyzing her? She was on a knife's edge between hope and despair. There *was* no hope, she reminded herself.

But still he'd brought her here. Why?

"I—" she began, but had no clue what she wanted to say. Then his words struck her. "Wait. Did you just buy this?" She pointed at the floor to indicate the house.

"I did. Would you like a tour? It's not a faithful restoration. It was gutted and modernized. I think you'll agree that's a good thing."

He offered his hand.

She hesitated, then moved as though in a trance, desperate for this small contact. This was how miracles worked, wasn't it? Without explanation? She took his hand, and the feel of his warm palm against hers as he interlaced their fingers nearly unhinged her knees.

"I thought you'd be angry with me," she said shakily. "About the letter." Each cell in her body was coming back to life.

"I am. But not with you. I'm angry that you had to write it. The kitchen." He identified the room with a wave as they walked into an airy space of cutting blocks and stainless steel, pots and pans suspended from the ceiling, and French doors that led to a patio herb garden. "The chef has yet to be hired, but you remember Fabiana? I poached her from the palace."

"Yes, of course. Hello," Amy greeted the maid. "It's nice to see you again."

"Ciao," Fabiana gave a small curtsy before she went back to putting away groceries.

"You can access the stairs to the terrace out there. You've seen the garden through the windows. Staff quarters are downstairs. Dining room, office, powder room, you've seen the main lounge," he said as he walked her through the various rooms, all bright and fresh and sumptuously decorated in a soft palette of rose and gray, ice blue and bone white. Shots of yellow and burnt orange, indigo and fern gave it life.

"It's a charming touch to keep this," she said as she paused on the landing to admire the window seat that looked over the road. "I can imagine call-ers waiting here to see if they would be allowed upstairs by the duke or—" *Prince*.

"There might have been a receiving room up here once, but it's all master suite now."

It was. There was a sumptuous yet intimate lounge with a television and a wet bar, a dining nook for breakfast and other casual meals, a beautiful office with floor-to-ceiling bookshelves and a fitness room that would catch the morning light. The actual bedroom was enormous, and the master bath had a walk-in shower, two sinks, a makeup vanity and…

"That tub!" Amy exclaimed as she imagined stepping into what was more of a sunken pool. It was surrounded by tropical plants and candles, begging for an intimate night in.

"I thought you would like it. Look at the closet." It had an access from the bathroom and was the size of a car garage. There was a bench in the middle and a full-length, three-way mirror at the back. Alongside his suits hung gowns and dresses and a pair of green pants with a mended fly.

It struck her then, why he'd bought this magnificent house. She'd seen the headlines since their breakup.

King's Mistress Dethrones and Departs

Whatever magic had begun to surround her flashed into nothing. She was left with singed nostrils, and a bitter taste in the back of her throat.

She twisted her hand free of his and stalked

through to the more neutral living area. Her adrenaline output had increased to such a degree that her limbs were twitching and her stomach ached. She couldn't decide if she wanted to spit at him or run to Baz Rivets again.

"I'm not making any assumptions," he began as he followed her.

"No?" she cried. "I won't live here. I won't be your—your *piece* in London, keeping your bed warm for when you happen to be in town."

"Stop it," he commanded sharply. "Think better of yourself."

His tone snapped her head back. He'd never spoken to her like that.

She folded her arms defensively. "I *am*."

"No, you're jumping to conclusions."

"What other conclusion is there?" She waved toward the closet.

In the most regal, pithy, arrogant way possible, he walked to a painting and gave it a light nudge to release a catch. It swung open, and he touched a sensor on a wall safe. It must have read his thumbprint because it released with a quiet snick.

He retrieved something before closing both the painting and the safe. Then he showed her a red velvet ring box and started to open it. "This was my grandmother's."

Amy was so shocked, so completely overwhelmed, she retreated in a stumble and nearly landed in an ignominious heap against the sofa.

She caught herself and managed to stay on her feet, then could only stare at him.

He gently closed the box. His expression became watchful, but there was tension around his mouth and a pull in his brows that was...hurt?

"As I said, I'm not making assumptions." He set aside the box—which made her feel as though he was setting her heart over there on a side table and abandoning it as he took a few restless steps, then pushed his hands into his pockets.

He snorted in quiet realization.

"Am I making another mistake? I don't like it," he said ironically. "I hurt you, Amy," he admitted gravely. "I know I did. I hate myself for it. Especially because I don't know that I could have prevented it. As long as you were interested in me, I was going to pursue you and we would have wound up where we did. That's been hard for me to accept. I don't like thinking of myself as having such a deep streak of self-interest."

He glanced at Amy for her reaction, but she had no words. He *had* hurt her. "I didn't exactly run away."

Until she had.

She bit her lip.

He nodded. "You hurt me when you left the way you did. That's not a guilt trip. I only want you to know that you can. I stood there telling myself I was doing us both a favor by letting you go, but I was so damned hurt I could hardly stand it."

"Nothing happened with Baz," she muttered.

"I know. He's a client and you don't have relationships with clients." He sounded only a little facetious. More of a chide at himself, she suspected. "It was genuinely shocking to me that anyone could hurt me so deeply just by standing next to another man, though."

She was reminded of their spat about jealousy when they were at his villa on the lake. When he had pointed out they were too new to have confidence in their relationship.

"I want you to come to *me* when you're hurt and scared and don't know what to do." He pointed to the middle of his chest, voice sharpening, then dying to sardonic. "And I want you by my side when *I* don't know what to do. I've hardly slept, I was trying so hard to work out how to spin things so you wouldn't be destroyed by all of this. I wanted to talk it out with you." He laughed at the paradox.

"And then I threw you under the bus," she said contritely, mentioning what was looming like a bright red double-decker between them.

"Don't apologize for what you wrote."

"I wasn't going to." But she clung to her elbows, deeply aware that she couldn't do that to a man and not have him hate her a little.

Which made her gaze go to the velvet box. Maybe it wasn't a ring. Maybe she *was* jumping to conclusions. How mortifying.

She jerked her gaze back to his, but he had seen where her attention had strayed.

"I want to marry you, Amy."

She ducked her face into her hands, all of her so exposed she couldn't bear it, but there was nowhere to hide.

"We don't even know each other, Luca!"

Gentle hands grazed her upper arms, raising goose bumps all over her body before he moved his hands to lightly encircle her wrists.

"I'm telling you what I want, that's all. What I know to be true. You don't have to answer me right now. I'll propose properly when you're more sure."

"What would our marriage even look like?" she asked, letting him draw her hands from her face. "We're not a match that people want to accept. We don't even live in the same country!"

"We can work all that out," he said, as if it was as simple as buying groceries. "My future is up in the air right now. The only thing I know for certain is that I want to be with you. So I bought a house here. We can date or you can move in. You can work or not. I'll get started with my own ventures. Maybe we'll move to Vallia at some point if it feels right. We can have a long engagement, so you have time to be sure. All of that is up for discussion, but I'd love for you to wear this ring when you're ready. I want people to know how likely I am to kill them if they malign the woman I love."

"You love me?" She began to shake.

"Of course, I love you."

"But you said…" She tried to remember what he'd told her about marriage. "You said you'd only marry someone vetted by… I'm not exactly the best choice of bride, Luca."

"If we make each other happy, that's all that matters. No. Wait," he corrected himself, cupping her face. "You are a bright, successful, badass of a woman who makes me a better man. How could anyone say that's a bad choice?"

"I make *you* better?" she choked out. "Hardly. You're perfect." It was annoying as hell.

"Exactly," he said with a shrug of casual arrogance. "I don't make mistakes. How could the woman I choose to spend my life with be anything but a flawless decision?"

"Oh, my God," she scoffed, giving him a little shove, before letting him catch her close. "You are a bit of a god, you know. It's intimidating." She petted his stubbled cheek before letting her hand rest on his shoulder.

"This is you acting intimidated? I can't wait until you're comfortable. You'll be hell on wheels once you trust me, won't you? Pushing back on me at every turn."

A pang of remorse hit her. "I should have trusted you and told you about Avery."

"It's a difficult subject. I understand."

"It wasn't just that," she admitted. "I was afraid of how you'd react. Afraid you would push me away and I would never have a chance to get to know you better. Then I was afraid you'd judge me. That I'd lose you." Her eyes dampened. "And then I did lose you."

"No, you didn't. I'm right here." A smile ghosted across his lips. "We had a fight, and we'll have others because we're both headstrong and used to thinking independently. But we'll always come back to each other. Wear my ring and I'll prove that to you."

"You really think we could make this work?"

"There's only one way to know."

"Okay." Nerves had her hand shooting out between them as though they were finalizing a deal. "I'll live with you here and—"

He yanked her close and swooped a deep kiss onto her lips, one that sent her arms twining around his neck in joy. One of her feet came off the floor.

He used the leverage of taking her weight to pivot her toward the bedroom door, then broke their kiss to walk her backward.

"Wait. I need more of that first." He paused and drew her properly against him, squeezing out all the shadows and filling her with a golden light while his mouth sweetly and lazily got reacquainted with hers.

They both groaned and she whispered, "I missed you."

She might have cringed then because it had only been a few days. They'd been dark ones, though. The beginning of eternity without him.

But here he was murmuring, "Me too," before sweeping his mouth across hers with more heat and passion and craving.

"Luca," she gasped as need sank its talons into her.

"*Sì*. I need you, too," he said in a rough voice and

picked her up to carry her through to the bedroom in long strides. When he set her on the bed, he came down with her and framed her face. "I need you, Amy. You. Never leave me again."

"Stay and fight?" she suggested on a shaken laugh.

"Sì." He pressed his smile to hers and they didn't talk again for a long time.

"Amy," Bea murmured. She and Clare widened their eyes with awe as they entered Luca's home several weeks later. Hers too, he kept insisting, but she was taking things slowish.

Not so slow that she didn't introduce Luca by his new title as she drew her friends into the lounge.

"This is Luca. My fiancé." She gave an exaggerated wave of her wrist to show off the ring. It was an oval ruby with a halo of diamonds on a simple gold band, not extravagant, but invaluable for its sentimental and historical significance. He had proposed properly the day she officially moved in with him. She'd been staying with him since he'd come to London so, even though it all happened very quickly, it felt right to make it official. She was beyond honored to be his future wife.

"Oh, my God! Congratulations." Bea and Clare hugged her nearly to death and grew flustered when Luca accepted their congratulations by brushing away an offer to shake hands and embraced each of them.

"I'm delighted to meet you both. And I look forward to getting to know you better, but Amy's been missing you. I'll let you catch up." He touched Amy's arm. "I'll tell my sister she can release the statement on our engagement."

"Thank you." Amy wrinkled her nose. She had asked him to wait on announcing it until she'd had the chance to tell her two best friends in person. "You spoil me."

"Nothing less than you deserve, *mi amore*." He set a kiss on her lips, nodded at the other two women and disappeared up the stairs.

Clare and Bea stood there with their mouths open.

"You've been busy," Clare accused.

"Oh, please. You both have plenty of explaining to do about your own whereabouts these last weeks. Come." Amy led them to where the wine and glasses were waiting. "Dish."

EPILOGUE

"AND THE WINNER for Most Innovative Integrated Media Messaging goes to London Connection, for their Consent to Solar Power campaign on behalf of AR Green Solutions."

Bea and Clare shot to their feet in excitement while Luca said a smug, "I knew it," beside Amy. He rose to help her out of her chair.

Amy needed help. She was eight months pregnant going on eleven. She had been on the fence about attending this ceremony, but it was her last chance for a night out and a rare opportunity to catch up with her best friends.

Of course, when they had planned it, Amy hadn't known she was pregnant again. It had been thrilling news to learn she was expecting their second child, but a surprise, considering it happened a mere twelve weeks after their daughter Zabrina had been born.

Despite how busy she was as a mother, Amy was keeping her hand in with London Connection. She had personally supervised the team who had come up with this promotion for the solar tiles Luca was producing with his partner Emiliano.

They were heading straight to Vallia in the morning, though. Sofia was not even engaged, let alone showing signs of producing the next ruler. This baby would be third in line for the throne after Luca and Zabrina. Everyone wanted this baby to be born there.

For the most part, Amy had been feeling good. Tired, but Luca was a hands-on father, and they had a nanny along with other staff who were always willing to cuddle a princess.

Even so, Amy leaned on Bea and Clare as they all went onto the dais. "Can you believe this is our life?" she asked them.

They were both beaming, all of them at the top of their individual worlds.

But as had always been their dynamic, both women gave Amy a little shove toward the microphone, letting her take the heat of the spotlight for all of them.

"I wouldn't be where I am without these two wonderful women beside me and the brilliant men who conceived these panels, most especially my husband who didn't dismiss me when I said 'What if we show your workers asking Mother Nature for consent?'"

A ripple of laughter went through the room at the unusual campaign.

"I'm the one who said she was out of her mind," Clare interjected, making Amy laugh because that was exactly what her friend had said, before assuring her she trusted her and encouraging her to go for it.

Something happened when Amy laughed, though. A release. She felt the flood of dampness and cringed with an agony of embarrassment.

"Ames?" Bea squeezed her arm. "What happened? Are you okay?"

"This is not a stunt for more publicity, I swear." Amy shaded her eyes and looked for her husband who was already moving quickly toward her, an anxious expression on his face. "But I'm about to make a scene."

"*Amore*, what's wrong?"

"I'm so sorry, Luca. My water broke."

As the whole room erupted, Luca gathered her into his side. "Of course, it did," he said ruefully. "Never a dull moment. Do you know how much I love you for that?"

Her love for him was touch and go for the next few hours while she labored to bring their son into the world, but at dawn, when she woke to see him cradling their newborn, her feelings toward him defied words.

He barely looked any worse for wear despite the fact he'd been up all night. His love for her and their son glowed from his expression when he noticed she was awake.

"Do you know how much I love *you*?" she asked.

"I think I do," he said, caressing her jaw and kissing her temple. "But tell me anyway."

* * * * *

Unable to put down
Ways to Ruin a Royal Reputation?

Look out for the next installments in the
Signed, Sealed... Seduced trilogy
coming soon from Clare Connelly
and Tara Pammi!

In the meantime, why not get lost in these
other stories by Dani Collins?

A Hidden Heir to Redeem Him
Beauty and Her One-Night Baby
Confessions of an Italian Marriage
Innocent in the Sheikh's Palace
What the Greek's Wife Needs

All available now!

WE HOPE YOU ENJOYED
THIS BOOK FROM
⟨H⟩HARLEQUIN
PRESENTS

Escape to exotic locations where passion knows no bounds.

Welcome to the glamorous lives of royals and billionaires, where passion knows no bounds. Be swept into a world of luxury, wealth and exotic locations.

8 NEW BOOKS AVAILABLE EVERY MONTH!

HPHALO2021

#3909 THE FORBIDDEN INNOCENT'S BODYGUARD
Billion-Dollar Mediterranean Brides
by Michelle Smart
Elsa's always been off-limits to self-made billionaire Santi. Now as her temporary bodyguard he'll offer her every luxury and every protection. To offer any more would be the most dangerous—yet tempting—mistake!

#3910 HOW TO WIN THE WILD BILLIONAIRE
South Africa's Scandalous Billionaires
by Joss Wood
Bay needs the job of revamping Digby's luxurious Cape Town hotel to win custody of her orphaned niece. That means resisting their off-the-charts chemistry, which is made harder when Digby gives her control over if—and when—she'll give in to his oh-so-tempting advances...

#3911 STRANDED FOR ONE SCANDALOUS WEEK
Rebels, Brothers, Billionaires
by Natalie Anderson
When playboy Ash arrives at his New Zealand island mansion, he never expects to encounter innocent Merle and their red-hot attraction. He's back for one week to lay his past to rest. Might he find solace in Merle instead...?

#3912 PROMOTED TO THE ITALIAN'S FIANCÉE
Secrets of the Stowe Family
by Cathy Williams
Heartbroken Izzy flees to California to reconnect with her past and finds herself in a business standoff with devastatingly handsome tycoon Gabriel. He's ready to bargain—if she first becomes nanny to his daughter...then his fake fiancée?

YOU CAN FIND MORE INFORMATION ON UPCOMING HARLEQUIN TITLES, FREE EXCERPTS AND MORE AT HARLEQUIN.COM.

HPCNMRB0421

SPECIAL EXCERPT FROM

Ⓗ HARLEQUIN
PRESENTS

*When Ares insists shy Bea accompany him to a gala,
she wants to refuse. The gorgeous Greek is as arrogant
as he is charming, yet she can't say no to her PR firm's
biggest client...or to one magical night in Venice!*

*Read on for a sneak preview of
Clare Connelly's next story for Harlequin Presents,*
Cinderella's Night in Venice.

As the car slowed to go over a speed bump, his fingers
briefly fell to her shoulder. An accident of transit, nothing
intentional about it. The reason didn't matter, though; the
spark of electricity was the same regardless. She gasped and
quickly turned her face away, looking beyond the window.

It was then that she realized they had driven through the
gates of City Airport.

Bea turned back to face Ares, a question in her eyes.

"There's a ball at the airport?"

"No."

"Then why...?" Comprehension was a blinding light.
"We're flying somewhere."

"To the ball."

"But...you didn't say..."

"I thought you were good at reading between the lines?"

She pouted her lips. "Yes, you're right." She clicked her
fingers in the air. "I should have miraculously intuited that
when you invited me to a ball you meant for us to fly there.
Where, exactly?"

"Venice."

"Venice?" She stared at him, aghast. "I don't have a
passport."

"I had your assistant arrange it."

"You—what? When?"

"When I left this morning."

"My assistant just handed over my passport?"

"You have a problem with that?"

"Well, gee, let me think about that a moment," she said, tapping a finger to the side of her lip. "You're a man I'd never set eyes on until yesterday and now you have in your possession a document that's of reasonably significant personal importance. You could say I find that a little invasive, yes."

He dropped his hand from the back of the seat, inadvertently brushing her arm as he moved, then lifted a familiar burgundy document from his pocket. "Now you have it in your possession. It was no conspiracy to kidnap you, Beatrice, simply a means to an end."

Clutching the passport in her hand, she stared down at it. No longer bothered by the fact he'd managed to convince her assistant to commandeer a document of such personal importance from her top drawer, she was knocked off-kilter by his use of her full name. Nobody called her Beatrice anymore. She'd been Bea for as long as she could remember. But her full name on his lips momentarily shoved the air from her lungs.

"Why didn't you just tell me?"

He lifted his shoulders. "I thought you might say no."

It was an important clue as to how he operated. This was a man who would do what he needed to achieve whatever he wanted. He'd chosen to invite her to this event, and so he'd done what he deemed necessary to have her there.

Don't miss
Cinderella's Night in Venice,
available May 2021 wherever
Harlequin Presents books and ebooks are sold.

Harlequin.com

Love Harlequin romance?

DISCOVER.

Be the first to find out about promotions, news and exclusive content!

Facebook.com/HarlequinBooks

Twitter.com/HarlequinBooks

Instagram.com/HarlequinBooks

Pinterest.com/HarlequinBooks

YouTube.com/HarlequinBooks

ReaderService.com

EXPLORE.

Sign up for the Harlequin e-newsletter and download a free book from any series at
TryHarlequin.com

CONNECT.

Join our Harlequin community to share your thoughts and connect with other romance readers!
Facebook.com/groups/HarlequinConnection

HSOCIAL2021